Justin was gone. . . .

The squall struck. The sail filled. The boat rolled far over, throwing Grace violently against the side of the cockpit. An eerie howl from below, Mooch afraid. Water everywhere, in warm drenching sheets from the sky, in cold explosions from the waves crashing over them.

The mast was tilted at an impossible forty-five-degree angle. And from it Justin hung by one hand, far out over the raging water. Lightning cracked and in the brilliant, blinding glare Grace saw him reach with his other hand to hold on, miss, claw wildly at the air, miss again.

"Justin!"

A second flash of lightning, the mast stark against electric clouds. Justin was gone.

"Justin!" Grace screamed again. A wave crashed over the boat, propelling it rudely forward, swamping Grace again. She clawed her way to a life buoy and hurled it against the wind into the sea. She snatched at the locker and began tossing orange life jackets overboard.

She screamed his name again and again into the darkness, her voice drowned by wind and rain.

But the only answer was more lightning, more wind, and Mooch's frightened wail.

Look for these other titles in the
Ocean City series:

Ocean City
Love Shack
Fireworks
Boardwalk

And don't miss
Boyfriends and Girlfriends,
Katherine Applegate's
romantic new series!

#1 Zoey Fools Around
#2 Jake Finds Out
#3 Nina Won't Tell
#4 Ben's In Love
#5 Claire Gets Caught
#6 What Zoey Saw
#7 Lucas Gets Hurt *

* coming soon

OCEAN CITY
REUNION

Katherine Applegate

HarperPaperbacks
A Division of HarperCollins*Publishers*

HarperPaperbacks   *A Division of* HarperCollins*Publishers*
10 East 53rd Street, New York, N.Y. 10022

Copyright © 1994 by Daniel Weiss Associates, Inc.,
and Katherine Applegate
Cover art copyright © 1994 Daniel Weiss Associates, Inc.

Produced by Daniel Weiss Associates, Inc.,
33 West 17th Street, New York, New York 10011.

First printing: July 1994

Printed in the United States of America

HarperPaperbacks and colophon are trademarks of
HarperCollins*Publishers*

10 9 8 7 6 5 4 3 2 1

Many thanks to K.J. Adams for her work in preparing this manuscript.

ONE

"Tears, idle tears, I know not what they mean. . . ."

"Typical poet," muttered Kate Quinn. After admitting in the first line that he didn't know what the tears meant, he spent nineteen more discussing the matter. Why had she chosen to do her paper on Tennyson? She needed a lighter poet—like Dr. Seuss.

Kate jumped up from her desk and paced around the dorm room. It was that line near the end of the poem that had suckered her in. "Deep as first love, and wild with all regret." The moment she'd read it, she'd felt it. There, in the middle of English 201, all of last summer had come rushing back to her.

And now the weather, this first April evening in New York, wasn't helping any. The air felt soft and warm and wet. Closing her eyes, it was easy for Kate to imagine herself back in Ocean City.

1

She leaned on the windowsill, her straight blond hair falling forward over her shoulders. In the twilight she could see the dome of Columbia's library and the outlines of the quad buildings sharp against the sky. No stars. If one wanted to make a wish here, best to wish upon the first pink blur of a streetlamp.

She gazed at the lamp beneath her window. What should she wish for?

"The days that are no more."

It was the refrain to Tennyson's poem, and it had been haunting her since this morning. Kate had awakened exhausted by a dream she could barely remember—except that there was ocean in it. It was the feeling of the dream that she strongly recalled, the sense of foreboding that had increased steadily during the day.

She longed to call her best friend, Chelsea, but what would she say—she'd had a dream she couldn't remember, she couldn't stop thinking about Justin, and she had this feeling that something terrible was going to happen? Chelsea had her own, real problems to deal with; marriage, for one.

"I've got two papers and four exams to study for," Kate said aloud, trying to focus. "And it all has to be done in the next three weeks."

Well, Tosh had said he'd help her. Tosh! She had completely forgotten about him. Snatching up her sweater and books, she turned to the door, then stopped.

2

"So. I am noticed at last." He leaned against the frame, grinning at her. But there were little lines in his brow, lines of concern.

Tosh McCall was one of the nicest surprises of Kate's freshman year. She had met him in her first-semester political-science course, for which he was a teaching assistant. Later he had complained to her that she hadn't glanced at him, hadn't deigned to acknowledge his existence—until she ran into trouble researching her final paper.

Truth was, all the girls in her poli-sci class had noticed the tall, brown-haired guy with intensely blue eyes. He looked great in tweed jackets, thin enough to appear academic, but strong enough—everyone knew—to cream his competitors on the squash court. The day he was allowed to lecture, there was perfect attendance, but not a lot of notes taken by the female members of the class.

So Kate had noticed all right, but, well, she'd had other things on her mind. And it wasn't until December that she had looked directly into those brilliant eyes. She had gone to the poli-sci department to check the bulletin board where final grades were listed. He was waiting for her there.

"Well, Quinn comma Kathryn," he said, mimicking the way her name appeared on class lists. "Being a man of honor, I have waited till the semester is over. It's over. Have lunch with me. Now!"

Kate had smiled then and smiled now.

"I like that look better," said Tosh, still leaning against her door. "Why were you smiling?"

"I was remembering."

"Oh." The light went out of his eyes.

"Remembering *you*," she said. "Remembering you last December."

"Oh!" He stepped inside the room. A guy went screeching down the hall. Two girls with water pistols chased him. Tosh closed the door, then crossed the room to Kate. He took her face in his hands and kissed her lightly, sweetly, a kiss like the touch of petals in spring.

Kate couldn't help it—she pulled back.

Tosh let her go, stared at her for a long minute, then stuck his head out her window.

"What?" she said, as he turned his head left and right.

"I'm looking for him," Tosh replied.

"Looking for who?"

"Him. Your knight. When I came in, you were standing here by the window like the Lady of Shalott. You remember the poem." He pointed to the book of Tennyson that lay open her desk. "The lady leaves her work, the tapestry she's weaving, to gaze at the handsome knight passing beneath her window. Perhaps he was *sailing* beneath her window," Tosh added bitterly.

Kate said nothing. She was sorry she had ever told Tosh about Justin.

"The knight, bold and gallant fellow that he is, is totally unaware of the lady and her feelings," he went on. "You know the story's ending, Kate. It isn't happy."

Kate bit her lip. She knew it well: the tapestry flew out the window—all the woman's dreams, all her work, gone.

But Kate hadn't let that happen! At the end of last summer, Justin had chosen his way, and she had chosen hers. "How dare you, Tosh, if you—"

"I'm sorry, Kate. Sorry," Tosh said quickly. "I shouldn't have said that. Jealousy is never charming." He walked away, his cheeks coloring a little.

"I'm sorry too," Kate replied, her voice softer now. "I don't know what's wrong with me this evening. I—I just feel so jittery."

Tosh sat down on her bed, then patted the mattress. "Come here."

She hesitated, then joined him.

"Lie down," he told her. "Come on, Kate," he urged, "this will be good for you."

She stretched out.

"On your tummy," he said.

Kate rolled over and he began to scratch her back. Slowly she relaxed. She felt like a child, safe, loved, her back being rubbed softly to coax her into sleep.

Kate wasn't sure how long she slept. When she woke up, Tosh was lying next to her on the narrow bed, reading.

She watched his long lashes as his eyes flicked across the page. She was tempted to reach out and touch his face. Here was a person with goals, dreams—other than sailing away from it all.

Here was a man sailing into the future, juggling a teaching schedule with graduate courses of his own and a part-time job. Maybe he couldn't drag swimmers from a pounding surf, but there was a quiet kind of heroism in how he lived his life.

He must have felt her looking at him. He glanced over. "Hi," she said.

"Oh, it's you."

She smiled, and he kissed the smile. Then he put aside his book and kissed the neck below the smile.

Then his hand slipped under her T-shirt and around her back. His mouth found her mouth again, with soft, deep kisses. He shifted his weight. Suddenly he was heavy on her. Suddenly there was no air, no light, only him on her and she was drowning, drowning.

She pushed him away.

He looked surprised—whether by her strength or the action itself, she wasn't sure.

"He's still between us, isn't he?" Tosh asked.

"Good old lifeguard man, who gave not a thought to coming with you, but asked you to give up your dream and come with him."

She didn't reply.

He sat up. "Why, Kate? Why this stupid loyalty? How often has he written to you since he left?"

She curled up her fist. "It's hard to find a mailbox in the middle of the ocean."

"Surely you don't entertain the fantasy that he is remaining loyal to you. . . ."

Was that a statement or a question? she wondered.

"For nine months he travels with his old girlfriend, Greta—"

"Grace."

"—in very close quarters," he went on. "Men have their needs."

Kate's eyes sparked. "And how do you think it is for women?"

"I've been waiting for you to tell me," he said.

She felt the heat of his hand on her thigh and turned away. "I have a paper to write, Tosh."

"Kate! Be honest with me. I can't stand polite lies. Just say it: Go away! Say it out loud: There's no room for me in your heart."

"But I do have to write this paper," she insisted, going over to her desk.

She heard his sigh behind her, then the creak of the bed as he rose from it. When he was outside the door, she added softly, "And I don't know if there's room in my heart."

"If you had to do it all over again," Justin wondered aloud, "would you?"

Grace Caywood didn't reply right away. She lay back on the cockpit bench, letting the Caribbean wind run its fingers through her dark hair, drying it.

She was looking for constellations—her favorite connect-the-dot pictures in the sky—but the stars were swimming too fast in and out of clouds. Funny, in eighteen years of living in Ocean City, where the sky was almost half of all she saw, she had never really looked at them. Evening, on that skinny strip of island, was when the boardwalk lights glowed. But in the last nine months Grace had watched the stars from the deck of Justin's boat, a glittering map shifting with the seasons and the latitude. North to Massachusetts they had sailed, then east to the Azores and in and out of Mediterranean ports. Now she and Justin were crossing back again. She had learned to read and love the stars: stars weren't just for wishing on, they were there to travel by.

"Would I do it again, captain, my captain?" she asked, smiling at Justin. His dark, penetrating eyes glimmered at her. Not many girls could say no to such an invitation.

"Oh, God!" Grace sat straight up, putting her hand over her nose. She pointed to Justin's dog, Mooch, who was riding stern. "Only if you trade in that behemoth for a chihuahua."

"Good dog," Justin said calmly. Mooch wasn't the brightest of mutts. Even after months at sea, it was a good idea to positively reinforce his potty training. Justin eyed the mess Mooch had made on the stern. "Your turn," he reminded Grace.

She curled her lip in disgust. "Look how big it is! How does he do it?"

"He eats bananas."

"Bananas! All of them?"

"'Fraid so."

Grace let out a hiss. Mooch's wagging tail drooped. His brown ears would have, except that they were perpetually flopped. "Why does he always eat the *fresh* food?" After months on shipboard, she yearned for anything that didn't contain some kind of preservative.

"Because he's still struggling to master the can opener," Justin replied.

"When is he going to learn ship rules?" she continued.

"Speaking of ship rules, Grace, you know we're conserving fresh water."

She fingered her damp hair. Not exactly cream-rinse silky, but clean. And her legs were tan and smooth. Yes, she had learned the art of shaving on a rolling boat.

Justin, on the other hand, hadn't bothered with a razor. Gone was his all-American, clean-shaven lifeguard look. Oh, the shoulders were still broad, and his body carved with muscles, but the dark beard must have held a pound of salt.

"You're getting as scruffy as Mooch. Soon I won't be able to tell you two apart."

"I'm the one who still uses the head," he said, referring to the boat's toilet. "Speaking of which, it was your turn to clean it. Three days ago."

"Yes, Mother."

"Maybe that's the problem," Justin said irritably. "Your mother never taught you responsibility."

Grace's green eyes flashed at him.

"I know your mother never made you clean the toilet," he added.

Well, of course not. First of all, Grace's mother was too busy peeing or puking in it; alcohol did that to you. Second of all, there had been maids. Maids. Marble tile. Sunken bathtubs. Furry bath mats. Soft-as-peach-fuzz toilet paper. Ahhh!

And it had been a living hell. That's why Grace had walked out of her mother's condo last summer, why she had moved into a tumbledown house with four strangers. That's why, last August, when housemate Kate chose to head north for college, Grace headed north and east on *Kate*.

Kate the girl and *Kate* the boat, the two great

loves of Justin's life. Grace smiled to herself. She wondered which Kate would go further. Both were ambitious little shi—uh, ships.

Grace looked for a star to wish on for her brother, Bo. Good wishes, that's all she had to send to Bo and David, the two loves of her own life. She felt a little guilty for it, for rushing off to see the world. But she'd be back to them soon.

The stars were being swallowed up fast tonight, she noticed. Sometimes the night seemed so hungry.

Whistling to herself, Grace stood up to fetch the bucket and wash away Mooch's mess. A malicious wave sat her back down again. A cross-sea was building. In the months at sea, Grace, who had endured several bouts of seasickness, had acquired some expertise in the matter of waves.

"Damn." Justin came racing up from below. "Barometer's dropping like a rock."

"Which is . . . bad, right?" Grace guessed.

"How many months has it been, Grace? Yes, dropping is bad, rising is good."

"Starboard is right and port is left. Bow is front and stern is back." Grace smiled winningly, but Justin wasn't buying. He was wearing his terribly responsible 'I'm the Captain' look.

"Just a small, localized disturbance, probably," he said, talking mostly to himself. "Still, it could be nasty. Grace?"

"Yes?"

"I'm going to reduce sail and rig lifelines. You go below and make everything secure. You know the routine. Mooch, you too. Below."

Grace did indeed know the routine. In the Mediterranean, they'd endured a fairly terrifying storm that had cost them a sail and had left Mooch badly battered by unsecured cans of food tossed around the cabin like ricocheting bullets. He was still frightened of storms.

Mooch raced below obediently, but just then Grace noticed an odd, strangely mesmerizing phenomenon—a phosphorescent white line, well out at sea, but moving toward them. It took several seconds before she realized it was rain, falling in sheets. Just a few hundred yards away a gray wall of rain was falling with such force that it flattened the sea.

"Son of a bitch," Justin said, sounding awe-struck.

"What is it?"

A stiff, cool breeze caught her hair and stood it straight out behind her. The wall of water advanced with terrifying speed.

"Squall line. Lash the tiller!" Justin yelled. "I have to lower the mainsail and hope to hell we can rig a storm jib." He pointed his finger at her for emphasis. "Get a life jacket on. Now! And hold on."

He leapt to the mast. Grace fell as much as jumped to the tiller, disengaged the autopilot, and fumbled clumsily with wet ropes, invisible in the darkness. A glance at the sea showed the squall hurtling down on them. The breeze was blowing harder still, as if the wind itself was racing to escape that deadly wall of water.

A curse from Justin.

"What? What is it?"

He was already climbing the mast, hand over hand up the tiny handholds. "Got a slider stuck," he grunted.

The sail was not coming down. The boat was turning away from the wind, but far too slowly. When the squall hit the big triangular sail it would lay them over on their side. Already they were heeling far over.

"Justin!" Grace screamed. He was thirty feet above the deck, clinging to the mast, working furiously at the stuck slider.

"Got it!" he yelled.

The sail shivered and began to fall. Too late.

The squall struck. The sail filled. The boat rolled far over, throwing Grace violently against the side of the cockpit. An eerie howl from below, Mooch afraid. Water everywhere, in warm drenching sheets from the sky, in cold explosions from the waves crashing over them.

The mast was tilted at an impossible forty-five-degree angle. And from it Justin hung by one hand, far out over the raging water. Lightning cracked and in the brilliant, blinding glare Grace

13

saw him reach with his other hand to hold on, miss, claw wildly at the air, miss again.

"Justin!"

Slowly, slowly the boat righted itself and turned from the wind.

A second flash of lightning, the mast stark against electric clouds. He was gone.

"Justin!" Grace screamed again. A wave crashed over the boat, propelling it rudely forward, swamping Grace again. She clawed her way to a life buoy and hurled it against the wind into the sea. She snatched at the locker and began tossing orange life jackets overboard.

She screamed his name again and again into the darkness, her voice drowned by wind and rain.

But the only answer was more lightning, more wind, and Mooch's frightened wail.

TWO

Chelsea Lennox climbed the last turn of steps, breathing hard. Oh, the joy of a fourth-floor walk-up!

When she and Connor found the apartment last September, they thought it was a bargain—by New York standards, of course. "Not only is each month's rent less than the cost of a trip to China," Chelsea had said, "we won't have to buy a Stairmaster."

Of course, that was when its living room/kitchen and bedroom looked larger than two walk-in closets with a doorframe in between. Funny how big a room can seem when there's no furniture in it, or paintings or fabrics or charcoal studies, or books or typewriter or cooking gadgets, or a tall Irish guy, or a slightly plump black girl, both of whom were used to having their own space.

Chelsea sighed. Her right arm ached with the awkward weight of a painting. Wrapped in protective plastic, it continually slipped through her fingers. Her left arm struggled with a stack of books, a swinging bag of groceries, and a plant. It was possible that this plant was demonic. With each flight of steps, it had grown heavier in her hand; besides which, it was the ugliest piece of vegetation she had ever seen, kind of hairy and sharp. That's why she had bought it. As soon as she spotted it, she knew that no one else would offer it a home.

Well, she could always stick it out on the fire escape.

It was the painting that she was really worried about, the latest masterpiece from her studio art course. This one would have to be nailed to the ceiling; there was simply no more wall or floor space.

She hoped there wouldn't be another fight. Then she looked above the horizon of the ratty fourth-floor carpet and saw the door of their apartment flung wide open. Two people in blue uniforms stood inside.

At first Chelsea's heart raced wildly. For all the squabbling between her and Connor in the last few months, she was ready to rush in there, throw her arms around her crazy redhead, and dare the police officers to drag him away. Reflex action. They were married; Connor was legal. No one could deport him now. Nonetheless, she hurried through the door. "Connor?"

"Chels."

"What's going on?"

"You mean it wasn't you who reported me?" he asked.

She stared at him. Then he smiled that quirky smile of his, though there wasn't much humor in it tonight. "We've been robbed."

Chelsea blinked. Then she dropped her books on the chair, set her plant on Connor's desk, hung her jacket on a lamp, and rested her painting in the space between the refrigerator and the ironing board.

"What was taken?"

"That's what we're trying to determine, ma'am," one of the officers replied.

"They thought, perhaps, the place had been ransacked," Connor said. "I told them no, this is how it always looks."

Chelsea bit her lip. Then she asked, "If you don't know what has been taken, how do you know we've been robbed?"

He pointed. "Larry King is missing."

Connor liked to watch the TV talk show host during dinner. With Chelsea's and his schedules so jumbled up by classes and work, they rarely saw each other for meals. Just as well, thought Chelsea; less time to fight.

Then she gazed at the nice empty niche,

which her newest painting had just settled into. Yup, Larry was gone, antennae and all.

"The clock radio left with Larry," Connor added. "Did you have any cash lying around?"

"No cash," said Chelsea, "but I left my credit card . . . somewhere." She glanced worriedly around the room, then saw it gleaming on top of the kitchen counter.

"Aha!" She held it up. "Imagine that. Our burglar friend never found it."

"Probably gave up," she heard one of the officers remark.

The older of the two turned to Connor. "Tell you what, Mr. Riordan, we'll let you and your wife sort through things. If you notice anything else missing, just give us a call. Thanks for the tea."

Connor nodded. "Always pleased to entertain New York's finest."

When the door closed behind the police, he turned to Chelsea. "So," he said. With his Irish accent, it sounded like *sooo*. "So, dear, how was your day?"

"Fine, dear. And yours?"

They stared at each other tensely. They used to laugh when they mimicked old married couples.

Not anymore. Since she had married Connor, Chelsea felt as if she had aged years; she felt at least forty-two. But lately she had wanted to scream and pinch and cry and pout, as if she were eight. The proper age of nineteen seemed to have been lost forever. And yet . . .

She knew it was true: she'd rather lose "nine-teen" than Connor. She loved him—every quirky bit of him—and could not imagine being with anyone else. Life without Connor would lack color and shape.

He was glancing around the room again, at her jacket on the lamp, her painting flopped to-ward the ironing board, the plant next to his typewriter.

"Chelsea, what is that ugly thing?"

"In America, we call it a plant."

"Where did you buy it? The Little Shop of Horrors? Where's its mouth? Remind me not to cut my finger near it."

"It's going out on the fire escape," she said.

He frowned at it as she lifted it up. "By morn-ing it will have eaten all the other plants out there. All that will be left of the jungle is Huge-and-Hairy, and little bits of crockery."

Chelsea moved toward the open window next to the fire escape, then stopped suddenly, setting the plant down. "Is that how the intruder got in?"

"By way of *our* fire escape?" Connor asked. "Do you think cat burglars carry machetes with them?" He pointed to the front door. "There. That way. So much for our hardware store of locks."

Chelsea winced when she looked at the door, scarred as it was by marks of a determined intruder. All those brass and steel fixtures—they were supposed to have made her and Connor safe and secure. But nothing could really keep them so. She felt afraid for the first time. Then she felt furious. She started to shake.

Connor reached for her. "Chelsea. I'm sorry. I'm being a jerk." He wrapped his arms around her. "It's okay, Chels. We're okay. A television, a radio, they're nothing important."

She nodded, her face pressed hard against his shoulder. "Daddy will get us new ones," she said.

Connor stepped back from her. "Daddy will not."

"He'll understand," Chelsea said.

"Daddy will not!" Connor repeated.

"Well, I don't see why not—"

"Because, damn it, Daddy didn't marry me. I will not have him supporting me—"

"So, Ronald McDonald has given you a raise?"

"—any more than he has to," Connor finished.

"Well, then Daddy can give *me* the television. I'll let you watch it occasionally."

"I'd think you'd have more pride than that," Connor growled.

"I'm sick of your Irish pride!"

"And I'm getting bloody tired of my African-American queen!"

They stared at each other for a full minute; then he turned away.

"Connor, what's wrong?" she asked. "We love each other. We have the encouragement of friends and the support of my parents. We're following our dreams—"

"You are," he observed quietly.

"And you will be in time," she reminded him. "We have more than a lot of people our age. Why do we act like this?"

He shook his head. "I don't know, Chelsea. Maybe we're just getting used to each other."

"We were getting used to each other in September!"

He put a quieting hand on her. "Then maybe we're getting used to each other growing."

She clung to him. "But what if we grow apart?"

"You mean, what if you become a world-famous artist, summering in the south of France, wintering in Aspen, spending your fall and spring in New York galleries and Paris salons, surrounded by admirers and intellectuals and all the beautiful people—well, then, I guess I'll just have to feed myself to Huge-and-Hairy here. Now I'm glad you've purchased him."

She grinned at Connor, then said, "But seriously, what if it happens to us, like it happened to Justin and Kate?"

"Well, it might."

She pressed her lips together. She had wanted him to say, *Oh, no, never, my darling!*

21

We will always be together. But Connor wouldn't. He had the soul of a poet, but the narrowed eyes of a cynic.

"Tell me," he said, "Do you think Kate regrets her summer with Justin?"

"She told me once she wouldn't give up that time for anything."

"So let's not give up *our* time for anything. Certainly not for first-year troubles."

Chelsea laid her head on his shoulder. "It seemed so simple at first. Girl meets boy in Ocean City. Girl marries boy in Ocean City. Girl and boy live happily ever after—"

"In New York?"

"We need to go back to Ocean City," Chelsea said. She closed her eyes, remembering the first time she saw Connor, the first time she touched him, the first time they kissed.

"Ocean City, Ocean City," Connor repeated softly. Then he kissed her so sweetly, she half-believed he knew the spell that could magically whisk them back there.

Grace glanced at the clock of the American Embassy office. Eleven thirty, and still dark out. Therefore, it was eleven thirty p.m. Therefore, it was the same night. But with the passing of the storm and a late moon rising, she couldn't shake the feeling that this was a new day, a new lifetime—a lifetime without Justin.

The Coast Guard had towed her in the last few miles. She had no voice to speak to them and, until they reached Nassau, sat on deck wrapped in a scratchy blanket. Their expert eyes took in the scene. One officer laid at her feet a yellow horseshoe, the only remaining floating device on board. It asked the question she couldn't yet answer out loud. Later she would tell them: she had thrown over everything else that might support a lost swimmer, as the wind rushed the boat away from him.

Instead she had said to the officer, "Try to imagine it. Me and Mooch sharing that little yellow ring."

Mooch had rested his head on her knee. He had a soaked-dog-and-ocean smell, and his fur was crusty. His chin was in the same place now, as they sat in an office that was empty of all but one consular official, who was taking down the accident information.

"Is that a dog, or has a huge barnacle attached itself to you?" the official asked.

Grace tried to smile. Her skin itched; it burned with salt. She longed for a drink and a huge bottle of moisturizer. "I don't suppose we could put your buddy outside for a bit?" the man asked. The smell clearly offended him.

"Not unless you put me out with him."

He nodded, and his fingers went back to tapping information into his computer.

If ever there was an excuse to start drinking again, Grace thought, this was it. She hadn't touched the stuff for ten months. Oh, but it would taste good! And surely, little weasely officials like this kept something in their desks.

"Do you have anything to drink?"

His eyes flashed away from the computer screen.

"Other than water and coffee," she added.

He leaned over in his chair, slid open a drawer, then set a bottle of scotch on the desk top. Straightening up, he eyed her, as he had when she had first walked in. But this time he let his eyes linger even longer. She was pretty sure the details he observed were not going into his report.

Then he put two glasses on the desk.

She waited for him to pour the lovely liquid. Justin would hate her for this. And David . . .

But Justin had more liquid in him than she could ever pour down her throat.

Justin was dead.

Dead.

And David, who knew, after nine months' time? He might have flown his little jet plane to the moon. Why should he stay around for her? He knew enough old drunks.

She should make calls. The drink would help her make the calls. It had always helped—the wonderful burning down her throat that told her

24

she was alive, and the satiny feeling that lapped her afterward. She remembered the feeling as if her last drink had been yesterday.

But already her brain was stumbling. Old drunks sometimes needed but one drink to be wasted again. If she couldn't talk on the phone, if she couldn't make herself clear the first time, she'd be telling the story over and over and over. She shut her eyes.

"Take it away," she said.

The official chuckled softly.

"Please."

There was a long silence.

"Please," she begged.

She heard the drawer open, and the clatter of glass. Even weasels had hearts, she thought.

"I have to make some calls," she told him.

The phone was pushed toward her. Grace picked up the receiver and tried to remember numbers. Home first.

When all the clicking, fizzing, and nose-pinched voices of operators stopped, the clear voice of her younger brother came on the line.

"Bo?"

"Grace. Gra-ceeey!" For him, her name was a word of celebration. She fought back the tears.

"Where are you?" he asked.

"The Bahamas. Nassau."

"Soaking up those rays, huh?"

She swallowed. "Listen, Bo, uh, where's Mom?"

"In her bedroom."

"*How's* Mom?" she asked.

Bo was quiet for a moment. In that moment, all the guilt she had felt for leaving her brother with an alcoholic mother washed over her like a fresh storm.

"Better—maybe."

"Maybe?"

"She went to her first A.A. meeting."

Grace was stunned.

"Came home cussing like—well, like you. Knows all the same words."

He laughed a funny-sad little laugh. Grace knew then that she couldn't tell him her bad news.

"How's Justin?" he asked.

"Justin?"

"Yeah, you know, the guy you went through school with, dropped out of school with, screwed around with, sailed away with—"

"Fine," she said. "Fine."

"Is everything all right?" Good old Bo. Even long distance with her faking it, he could still pick up some signals.

"Listen, Bo, I called to tell you I'm coming home soon."

"Are you? When?" It was there again, his younger voice, the voice of a kid who adored his big sister.

"Soon."

"Tell me when, Grace. And call from your last

port. I want to be there when you and Justin sail under the O.C. bridge."

Grace squeezed the phone. Tears were falling fast now. "I'll call. Soon. Later. Love you, Bo."

She hung up the phone. Mooch shifted his head, plunging it deeper into her lap. She snatched a napkin from beneath the doughnut on the official's desk and blew into it with a loud honk. The man glanced at her but said nothing. No doubt he wasn't finding her quite so attractive now.

Next call, Grace, she told herself. With grim determination she pulled the little telephone book out of her purse. The names looked blurry, but she found it. Kate the girl.

This time she'd have to tell the whole truth.

Afterward it was hard for Kate to remember what time the call came.

"Are you there, Kate? Are you there?" Grace kept asking as she recounted what had happened. "I'm telling you all I know, all right? I'm telling you all I know now, because I can't tell you it again. Are you there?"

Kate had nodded silently into the phone. Then, sometime after Grace had hung up, Kate did. But she continued to sit on the edge of her bed, for a few minutes, or a few hours—she wasn't sure.

They couldn't find him, Grace had said. They had to accept it, Grace had said. Justin was dead.

"Justin is dead," Kate whispered. "I'll never see him again." She stood up and told the news to the blue-eyed girl in the mirror, who looked back with the pale face of a ghost.

Then she put on her nightgown and robe and a pair of soft slippers and padded down the dorm hallway. No one was around. She walked into the shower and turned it on—both spigots, full force. The water came at her hard, like a spray of needles. She turning her face upward, letting the water fill her mouth and run up her nose, letting it burn in her eyes and swell her lids.

Everything washed out of Kate's mind but the water itself. She didn't hear the bathroom door swing open.

"Kate?" Chelsea's voice echoed strangely. "Kate, are you in there? . . . She's here, she's here! Kate's by herself, and she's dressed."

Then Kate heard deeper voices. She rested her face against the tile wall and kept her back toward them.

The water was shut off. Kate shivered in the sudden quiet. Her soaked robe hung heavy on her shoulders. Chelsea's hands reached around from behind and turned her slowly. Connor and Tosh stared at her.

"Justin's . . ." Kate began, then reached again for one of the spigots. Chelsea caught her hand.

Kate gazed at her friend, then tried the words once more. "Justin's dead."

"It appears that way," Connor replied gently.

"But they haven't found him," Chelsea added. "And you know Justin's a good swimmer, and there's always the slim chance—"

"Chelsea!" Tosh's voice was sharp and both Chelsea's and Kate's head swung toward him. "I know you're trying to help, but if you encourage those kinds of thoughts, it's just going to be harder for Kate in the end."

Chelsea pressed her lips together.

Kate looked up at the shower head, longing to turn it on again, to drown the world around her. Somehow she couldn't cry; she needed to let the shower rain down around her.

She turned it on hard and Chelsea jumped back. Then Tosh stepped forward. He turned the water back to a warm and gentle mist and stood under it with Kate, his arms wrapped around her. At last Kate began to cry.

THREE

The packers moved with startling efficiency. Bo and Grace's life, ten years of it, was being boxed up in eight hours.

Grace watched the workers with a coolness and detachment that she was certain fooled the lawyer. Genevieve Gugerty continued to set out papers on the coffee table, readying them for Grace's signature.

David was stealing glances at her; Grace knew that he wasn't fooled. He was the one who held her when she woke up screaming about the storm. He was the one who listened when she talked about her friendship with Justin. And three weeks later, he was the first she had called after the police told her that they had found her mother.

"We need you to come down and identify her," the policewoman had said.

"Oh, I can identify her from here. She's the drunk in the fine suit, silk scarf, and Cartier earrings."

But, in fact, her mother was the drunk in the birthday suit. Or perhaps it was her skinny-dipping suit. They had pulled her out of the ocean when it was too late to do anything for her.

The autopsy report showed a high level of alcohol in her blood. Her mother didn't know any other level, Grace had thought. The police theorized that she had gotten drunk and gone for a swim.

"Must have been a bit chilly," said Grace.

Somehow she had kept herself standing upright throughout the police visit, the identification of the body, and breaking the news to Bo. David, lucky guy, was there for the collapse.

"Swim away while you can!" she had warned him, when she couldn't hold back the tears any longer. "I've drowned two people in one month."

He'd gripped her by both arms, his brown eyes as liquid as hers. "You didn't drown anyone, Grace!"

"Yeah, well, I didn't save them either."

Now David stood by the window, his head of dark curly hair bent a little, listening to her and watching the storm outside. The nor'easter wrapped itself around the penthouse, making invisible the long strip of barrier island on which the condominium perched.

Bo was in his bedroom packing—he trusted no one else with his treasures. Also, Grace thought, he probably didn't want the packers to know that Soupy, a stuffed dog who still lived in the back of his closet, had to be wrapped most carefully.

"Just a few more signatures, Grace, and we'll be finished," Ms. Gugerty said. "How are you doing?"

Grace stared at the woman with fuzzy salt-and-pepper hair and heavy, black-rimmed glasses. Prim as an old schoolteacher, she thought. But that wasn't the reason Grace disliked her so. Ms. Gugerty was her mother's attorney, her mother's advocate, her voice from beyond the grave.

"Great. Why shouldn't I be great? I just inherited a couple million dollars."

Then David spoke up. "Gen knows your relationship with your mom was troubled. And she knows about your mother's drinking."

Gen? Grace looked suspiciously from David to the lawyer. "Oh, wonderful," she said at last. "Another drunk. I don't think I've seen you at the last few A.A. meetings. Don't tell me my mother's estate is being overseen by a lawyer who hops on and off the wagon."

"No," the woman said in an even voice, "by a lawyer married to a man who hops on and off the wagon."

"Gen and I know each other from Alateen," David interjected. "I told you I had started working with the kids this winter. Gen's the one who got me involved."

Grace swallowed. Often she had encouraged Bo to go to Alateen meetings, which were for children of alcoholics. He had always resisted, but she kept hoping. "Nice of you to help out others," she told the lawyer, though she still couldn't speak to her with any warmth in her voice.

"I do it for me," the woman replied.

Grace picked up her pen. "Well, let's get this over with."

Besides plenty of stocks, money market accounts, treasury certificates, and three beach houses, she was now the proud owner of the condo they sat in—and which she was clearing out of permanently. There were just too many memories here.

As if reading her mind, the lawyer said, "Have you given any thought as to where you would like to live?"

The woman knew that the furniture was going into storage, and that her and Bo's mailing address was David's.

"I don't see how it concerns you," Grace said stiffly.

Ms. Gugerty studied her for a moment, then said, "It does. In February your mother talked to me about you."

Here it comes, thought Grace.

"She worried about you—"

Grace sucked in her breath.

"—and figured that when you returned from your trip, you still wouldn't want to live with her."

"Well, she figured right," Grace said. "And you should have told her to worry about herself, not me."

"In fact, I did," said the lawyer. "But she didn't listen. Once a mother, always a mother, I suppose. I don't know—I never had children."

"I rarely had a mother," said Grace.

"In any case," Ms. Gugerty went on with her quiet, steady voice, "for the coming summer she rented out all of what are now your properties, except one. She kept that free, in case you wished to live there."

"Which one?" Grace asked, then regretted being so quick with the question.

"Landfall, I believe it's called."

"Landfall. Oceanfront, end of the boardwalk," said Grace.

"The house is rather large. Your mother said you had some new friends now."

"Damn her."

"And the place you lived in last year was . . . uh . . . run down."

"Damn her!"

"She thought you'd like the large bathroom in the master suite."

35

"*Damn* her!"

"And the fireplaces. She said you were a romantic at heart," said the lawyer. "Of course, if you don't wish to live there, we can always arrange for a rental. Even in May, there are people who'd jump at the chance to rent such a place."

"Only she," said Grace, pointing her finger at the lawyer, accusing her mother's representative, "only she could figure a way to keep me where she wants me. She, whose whole life was out of control, has always wanted to control mine. Only *she* could figure a way to continue to do it. God, and from beyond the grave! Well, she won't!"

"It's a great house," said Bo quietly.

Grace spun around. She hadn't heard her younger brother come in.

"I like Landfall," he said.

Grace glared at him, then turned back to the lawyer.

"Maybe she wanted to control you," the lawyer agreed. "Or maybe she wanted to provide for you. It's hard to determine exactly why human beings do what they do."

"You got that right, Lady Attorney."

"Well, you don't have to decide right now," Ms. Gugerty said, opening her briefcase and slipping the signed papers into various folders and files. "I think you've dealt with enough today. I certainly have," she added.

Grace saw David's sly grin.

"You'll be receiving copies," Ms. Gugerty went on. "I know you have my number, but here it is again. We'll be in touch."

The woman held out her hand. Instead of shaking it, Grace leaned over to pick up the business card. Then she watched as David acted the gentleman and escorted the lawyer to the door.

When she was gone, Bo walked over to his sister, standing close, but not too close, to her. "Who you angry at, Grace?"

"Don't be a little jerk."

"Who?" he asked again. "Remember, we used to wonder about that with Mom. Was it Dad? Was it us? Maybe she was just pissed at herself. But we could never ask her."

Grace sat down. If she hadn't, her knees would have given way. Her whole body felt as if she had been swimming through heavy seas. "I'm not angry at *you*, Bo."

"Not even if I tell you I really want to live at Landfall?"

Grace blinked, then shook her head no. "Not even. Do me a favor?"

"Sure."

"Let me be for a while."

"Sure, Gracie."

He walked backward, his face showing concern, then turned and disappeared.

"Me too?" David asked.

She looked over at him. "You've been so good to me, David. So understanding . . . Yes, you too."

Then she closed her eyes. Her arms and legs felt so heavy. Soon she was swimming again, though in the dark nightmare sea. It was difficult to tell whether it was toward or away from her drowning mother.

"What a day!" said Kate.

Tosh closed the door behind them. "I believe you like it here."

"Love it! All this green!"

"And all this wet," he said, staring out at the Connecticut woods.

Raindrops hung silver from every tree, and nearly every branch was tender with leaves. The misty air had a rich dirt smell. The ground was soft beneath their feet.

Tosh was right. She really had needed to get away from the city. But somehow, planning a weekend away with him, making a reservation for two, seemed to mean something more about their relationship than she was ready for—even if he meant what he said about separate beds.

Then the perfect excuse had come. Professor Rosenthal, Tosh's mentor, needed a house sitter while he attended a conference. His home, a cozy wooden house with walls of bookcases, a stone fireplace, and a well-stocked kitchen, was just a commuter ride from Columbia's campus.

Forty minutes on the train, and Kate and Tosh were in a completely different world.

Kate stretched, touching a pine branch, shaking down spring rain on her and Tosh. "I'm so glad I came!"

"No kidding," said Tosh. "You snored like a sow in sweet hay last night. I had to close the door between our rooms."

She looked into his teasing eyes. "Did not."

"Did too."

"Your door was open this morning," Kate said. "I'm certain."

"You mean when you came for a peek at me?" Tosh asked.

Kate's mouth dropped a little. Her cheeks grew warm. "I—I just wanted to see if you were awake," she explained, then started to walk.

"I was."

"Well, you could have said something."

"It was more fun letting you look," Tosh replied, "seeing how long you took to examine me. I was disappointed when you didn't check under the covers."

Kate's cheeks grew hotter, and she moved quickly ahead of him. She was glad that the path she chose was too narrow for them to travel side by side.

It was true: she had slept heavily enough to snore like a sow in sweet hay. It was the first time she had slept well since she received the news of Justin's accident. And when she had awakened early that morning, fresh from such a sleep, she lay back and remembered the day before. She remembered the long, sun-warm afternoon and the rainy evening that followed and the flurry of soft kisses by the fire. She thought about all the kind things Tosh had ever done for her.

Suddenly she had to see him. She had tiptoed into his room to look, just to look. Okay, maybe she did stay long enough to memorize him. . . .

Now Tosh caught up with her, his long stride overtaking hers. "Are those roses in your cheeks for me?"

"You egotistical male," she said, pulling away. Of course they are, she thought.

"If it makes you feel any better, I peeked at *you* last night," he told her.

"To see if the fairies had changed me into a snoring sow?"

"Oh, are there fairies in these woods? I knew there was magic. I thought the magic was you."

Kate turned her head so he could see her roll her eyes. "I don't know where you get some of your lines."

"You inspire them."

"Please," said Kate, "don't blame me for your clichés."

When she looked back again, he was smiling to himself.

She began to smile too.

They walked on silently, watching their footing, which had become tricky. The night of heavy rain had made the trail slippery with mud. Little stones rolled underfoot.

Silence was comfortable with Tosh. He was a guy who could happily work beside her, his arm a half inch from hers, thinking his own thoughts while she thought hers. With him, she had often felt at peace. That peace had been disturbed by Justin's death, but now she felt a feather of it once again.

"I'm glad I came with you," she said.

"Are you?"

They were climbing a ridge from which the land dropped away steeply to the left. There was a long, muddy slash in the hillside, where the rainwater had gullied down to a low-lying brook. The water below them gurgled noisily. "Listen to that stream," she said. "It's laughing."

"Because of the rain last night," he replied softly. "It laughs today as loud as it cried last night."

She turned to look back at him.

"Careful," he said.

Just as he spoke, her left foot slipped sideways. Kate reached out for a branch to catch herself. Tosh reached out for her.

The branch snapped. Now her right foot slid, too, and she heard Tosh swear. The next moment they were sliding down the hillside together, screaming, then laughing like crazy, two laughing, crazy kids in a mud chute. Mud sprayed everywhere—rushing at them, flying up her shorts and shirt, splattering her face and hair. Toward the bottom, where it was very steep, they started to tumble. She ended up on top of Tosh.

When she saw him blinking up at her through a mask of mud, she threw back her head and laughed again. Then, though they had stopped tumbling from the hill, they started rolling again, over and over, he on top of her, she on top of him, kissing, their mouths frantically searching and finding and searching some more. Then his shirt was off and they struggled with hers. Like two mud wrestlers they clung and rolled. And her mind rolled backward to Justin, Justin, Justin—oh no!—had she said it out loud?

But Tosh was still kissing her, with hot fervent kisses. She pulled back and slipped her hand between them, resting it gently on his mouth.

Tosh was shaking, quivering all over. He rolled off of her. "Him again."

She didn't say anything.

"Now that he's a ghost, he can show up anywhere," Tosh remarked bitterly.

"I'm sorry. *I'm sorry,* it's just—"

"And you know how it is with the dead," he said, "they always look better—more handsome, more loving, more thoughtful—with each passing day."

"Tosh!"

"Kate!" He looked into her eyes, then he sighed. "*I'm* the one who should be sorry. That was a heartless thing for me to say."

Whether it was anger or passion that was draining out of him, she wasn't sure.

"I just need some time," Kate told him.

"And I need you," he said. He gave a little shrug. "So take the time you need. I'm not wandering anywhere."

He helped her to her feet. She handed him his shirt, which was a vest of slime.

He buttoned it. "Do I look as beastly as you?"

She grinned at him.

They washed their faces and arms in the stream. Then he reached for her hand, almost shyly, she thought. They walked along the water and crossed a spot with stepping-stones. On the other side of the stream was a tree with a broad limb, perfect for sitting.

"Madam?" He gave her a boost up. "At such a romantic moment as this," Tosh said, eyes twinkling, "would you like to hear me sing 'Weekend in New England'?"

Kate swung her legs back and forth. "Do you sound anything like Barry Manilow?"

"As a matter of fact, quite a bit!"

"Forget it," she said.

43

FOUR

"Ow!" Grace tucked her arm in close to her side and continued walking through the sliding glass doors onto the terrace. When Marta's wheelchair had rolled through, Grace pulled the screen shut behind them. Then she looked back reproachfully at the metal frame. "You'd think in three weeks' time, I would learn where the walls and doors are in my own house."

In my own house. She had said it out loud; she had said it so naturally. Of course, Landfall was hers now.

"Don't tell the others how you've seen me bump around for the last twenty-four hours. You know I have an image to maintain. Everyone thinks I'm a put-together chick—at least, when I'm a dry one."

Marta smiled and tossed her head. The ocean wind teased out long strands of her dark curly hair. "You *are* a put-together chick," she replied, eyeing Grace in her bikini, an expensive one, made of dark blue material striped with thin gold threads.

Each of Grace's bathing suits, and there were many in her walk-in closet, had a coordinated cover-up that, Marta reflected, didn't cover up much of anything. The wrap with the thin gold stripes was now thrown casually over the back of Grace's lounge chair—except that whenever Grace tossed things casually, they landed just right. *Just right.*

Perhaps that was why Marta enjoyed watching her "landlady" bump around for a change. She laughed out loud when Grace walked into the newly installed chair lift and swore like a sailor. The lift was put in for Marta. She could roll her wheelchair into the house through the front door, then take the lift down to the lower level, where her bedroom was. Marta felt quite at home, though she had never lived in a house as large or elegant.

It was a beautiful place—three levels with all the space and light of a contemporary beach house, constructed of natural-looking gray wood.

"You know. You've seen them. Big and gray," Marta's father had said, after admitting that he had checked out the place. "It looks like they nailed some driftwood together, and halfway through ran out of it, so they filled in with a lot of glass. God help you, girl, if a hurricane comes through. It's got decks everywhere—you'd think you were on a damn boat."

Actually, it had just two decks. The first was on the upper level, a private deck off Grace's sumptuous bedroom. From there you could look east, straight out at the ocean, or south, down the boardwalk, which ended just before the property of Landfall. A larger deck ran the length of the middle level; the breakfast, dining, and living-room areas, fronted by floor-to-ceiling glass, shared its sweeping view of the ocean.

The lower floor, where Marta had her bedroom, was ground, or rather, sand level. Bo had also been offered a room down there, away from his big sister, but requested the garage instead. That allowed him to move directly from his bed to his skateboard to the world at large.

Along the back of the lowest level was the terrace, where Marta and Grace were sitting now, soaking up the sun, savoring the last few moments of peace before Memorial Day weekend. The only sounds they could hear were waves crashing, sea gulls screeching high above them, and the hammering of a single workman from somewhere along the boardwalk.

Grace hummed with contentment and smoothed oil down her arms, rubbing gently her right one. "I'm going to have to borrow one of those pads Bo wears for skateboarding," she said, "to protect this poor, abused elbow."

"Elbow," Marta repeated, tilting her head back to the sun's soothing warmth. "Joint between the humerus, radius, and ulna."

"Don't go medical on me," said Grace.

Marta smiled without opening her eyes. "Otherwise known as crazus bonus," she said.

"You really like it, don't you? All that biology and chemistry and math you had to take this year."

"I really like working with people who have medical problems," said Marta. "So I deal with all that bio and chem and math."

"Well, it's not for me," said Grace, "being inside a clinic all day with people that are bleeding and puking. How depressing!"

"Challenging!" Marta corrected her. "Sometimes it's like solving a mystery, figuring out what is wrong, what the person needs. And I love mysteries."

"So I guess that means you won't manage one of my beach stands?"

"No," said Marta, stretching her long, strong arms. "You'll have to find some other sucker to roast in the sun for minimum wage."

"I'll probably get all the runaway Tina Wina Tacos."

They both laughed, remembering Chelsea's first job last summer, when she dressed up as a huge taco and handed out coupons on the boardwalk.

"How many stands do you have?" asked Marta.

"Six. I've hired for five already, so I just need two more people. Keep an ear out at the clinic for some failed waitress or busboy. It's a great job. You get to see and be seen."

"Speaking of scenery," said Marta.

Grace stopped oiling her body. "Yes, yes, yes," she agreed, following Marta's eyes to a guy who stood at the end of the boardwalk, about fifty feet away from the terrace. He had turned his back on them just as Marta had spoken, but the glimpse she had gotten made her keep on looking.

"Love those broad shoulders," said Grace. "And cute buns, too."

"Come on, buddy," Marta said softly. "Turn around again, let's get the full effect."

As if he had heard her, the stranger turned toward the ocean, showing them his profile.

"Well!" said Marta. His black hair whipped back in the wind. His dark features seemed cut in stone against the blue sky.

"Nice," Grace murmured, then she reached for a pair of field glasses that Bo had left on the terrace.

"Grace!" Marta reached over to snatch the binoculars away from her.

"Hands off," said Grace. "You'll get your turn."

Marta laughed and sat back in her chair.

"Mmm," said Grace. "Mmm-mmm-mmm."

Marta had the feeling she was acting a bit for her sake, or just for amusement. Well, so what? she thought. What guy doesn't like to be looked at?

Apparently, this one. Or maybe he just didn't like to look at girls in wheelchairs.

He had turned suddenly and stared with wide-eyed surprise into the binoculars Grace held in front of her. Grace wouldn't drop the glasses, even after she had been spotted. Then his head jerked quickly toward Marta. Marta was still laughing, high on the sunlight and the boldness of Grace.

Suddenly she saw the stranger's features change. They seemed to be dissolving, the strength in his face deserting him. She turned away quickly. She did not wish to meet the look of someone who felt so sorry for her.

"Not that cute after all," she muttered.

When she finally glanced up again, he was gone.

Grace put down the binoculars. "What a strange look he had on his face. For a moment I thought he knew you. Did you see his expression?"

"I saw it," said Marta.

"I think I scared him away," Grace went on. "Wimp!" She lifted the glasses again and began scanning the beach in front of them.

I scared him away, Marta thought, but she didn't say it out loud. She was glad that it didn't occur to Grace that the young man's strange look was one of pity or, perhaps, embarrassment. It didn't occur to Grace that that was how many people responded to Marta; they had since the shooting, seven years ago.

She could always guess what they were thinking: "Such a pretty girl! What a shame." And the guys: "She's got boobs, nice boobs. But the chair."

Marta bit her lip. Stop it, she told herself. She didn't usually indulge herself with this sort of bitter thinking.

Besides, not all guys were like that. Alec wasn't. He had seen her withered legs; he knew every inch of them. He had loved her. Too bad she had decided she didn't love him.

"Starboard, Marta!"

Marta's head bobbed up and she looked to the right. "My, my," she said appreciatively.

"Does this mean we're in the market again?" Grace asked as they watched two hunks stride down the beach.

"*We?*" Marta replied with a raised eyebrow. "Does this mean *David* is free? May I have him?"

"Not unless you want me to tear out each strand of your lovely black hair."

"Oh well." Marta smiled.

"So, you really are free?"

"I told you yesterday, Grace. Alec and I are friends now, nothing more."

Grace nodded. "I thought you might just be saying that. I was afraid you were disappointed because he opted for that internship in Washington."

Marta shook her head. "I think I'm relieved. Not that I don't care for him. We will always be friends."

"That's fine. Just friends. He wasn't for you, Marta," Grace said with certainty. "Though I will admit he had the face and yellow hair of an angel, and the body of a god."

"Ah!" Marta agreed. "I can see him now, melting hearts in the hallways of the Capitol, jogging around the Mall, a string of pretty congressional aides following close behind."

"Let them! You need more than that," said Grace.

"Now wait a minute!" Marta replied, suddenly feeling the need to defend him. "Alec has a brain. He's no dumb blond."

"Maybe," Grace replied, "but he lacks a certain . . ." She waved her hand around vaguely.

"Mystery?" Marta suggested.

"You look at a guy like him," Grace continued, "and you think: White bread."

"Tofu."

"Wholesome."

"Bland."

"Of course," said Grace, "fooling around with a man of dark mystery can be playing with fire.

Take it from one who's been there. You might eventually find out something you wish you never knew."

"Well, if I find a man of dark mystery, I guess I'll just have to take my chances," said Marta.

Grace tilted her chair all the way back. "Haven't you always?"

"I see it! I see it!" Chelsea shouted from the back of Kate's red convertible.

"We hear you, we hear you," Connor muttered from the front.

Kate slowed down as she approached it: the Ocean City bridge. To Justin, looking up at it from the water last summer, the bridge's low arches made a little gateway to the great world beyond. To Kate, who viewed it from above, it had been a road that led to and then away from Justin. Now where was it taking her?

"Ocean City! Just like I remember it!" Chelsea said.

Connor glanced over at Kate. "You'd think she was returning to the mother country."

Kate shrugged. There was something about Ocean City that made it seem like a country to itself. This long, sandy scrap of land, with its wooden houses and old hotels crammed together at one end, and its tall, honeycombed condos towering absurdly at the other, had its own personality. Beautiful and gaudy, Ocean

City was definitely its own place.

Kate was glad she had decided to return. She'd had doubts about it when Grace first invited her. Those doubts had grown on the way down from New York. The constant bickering between Chelsea and Connor had set her on edge and made her wonder just what kind of a summer everyone was in for.

But now she was here, driving the highway that ran north, straight up the middle of the island, and seeing all the old sights: the bike shop, the weathered church, Dilly's Taffy, Moondoggie's Golf. Now she remembered: there were memories here other than those that belonged to Justin.

Kate was so busy looking, she missed Grace's street. Under Connor's direction, she made a U-turn where a sign said No U-Turn, and at last pulled up the driveway that curved in front of Grace's house.

The front door opened immediately. Kate was momentarily stunned, both by Grace's beauty—she had forgotten how glamorous she was—and by the ease with which she played her new role, welcoming them as mistress of the house.

Connor took it all in stride. "We would have been here earlier," he said, hopping out of the car. "But we had to pay tribute to Vince Lombardi, Joyce Kilmer, and other illustrious Americans along the turnpike. It was inspiring,

Grace. One day, if I keep working hard enough at my writing, I too may get a rest stop named after me. Is this a great country, or what?"

He turned to Chelsea, who was still sitting in the backseat, looking like a kind of parade queen, enthroned on garbage bags, stuffed pillowcases, mesh grocery bags, and piles of magazines.

"Shall I unpack you now, dear?" Connor asked.

"I can get out myself," Chelsea snapped. "I'm just taking the time to look."

She and Kate stared up silently at Grace's house.

"It's beautiful," said Kate, her eyes lighting on the long sloping roof of the street side of the house, the large chimneys, the very contemporary and rather elegant entrance.

"Yes, we've come a long way from bayside," said Connor. "Where's Jethro and Ellie Mae?"

Grace laughed.

"Marta!" Kate exclaimed, happy to see her rolling out the front door.

"You sure are loaded down," Marta observed.

Kate and Connor immediately turned to Chelsea, who was climbing out by way of the convertible's trunk.

"So aren't there going to be any hugs?" asked Chelsea.

"Why, that's just what I was thinking," said

Connor. "I'm glad Alec . . . isn't here." He had caught himself just before saying "Alec and Justin." He blustered: "I'll take on his responsibilities, two warm embraces for each lass. That's all right, isn't it, dear?"

"Would you stop calling me 'dear'!" Chelsea snapped.

Grace caught Kate's eye. Kate turned away. She knew Grace was wondering about the status of Chelsea and Connor's relationship, but she wasn't eager to talk about it. Or, perhaps, she wasn't eager to talk to Grace. Kate hadn't counted on it being difficult to see her again. She hadn't counted on the questions and doubts that were now rising up in her mind.

"So you two will be right next door," said Marta.

"Yes," said Connor. He pointed to a tired-looking, wooden apartment building. "We will be in the efficiency at the back of—the Love Shack," he said, recalling the name Kate's father had given to their house last year. "Right next door to you at Love Manor."

"It's called Landfall," said Grace.

"I'm still waiting for my hugs," said Marta.

Then hugs went all around, and Connor wasn't the only one getting two from each person. There was some sniffling and wiping of eyes.

In the midst of it, a BMW convertible with a license tag reading "Gracie" purred up the drive.

David opened the door and stepped out quickly. "I see I arrived just in time," he said. The hugging began all over again.

Then Kate glanced over her shoulder. She saw Bo sitting patiently in the front seat of the car. "Hey, Bo!"

He grinned and waved at her. She guessed that he wasn't getting out of the car until all this fussing stopped. Then she saw some movement in the seat behind him. With the reflections off the windshield, she couldn't tell what it was.

"Did you and Bo bring someone else?" she asked David.

"We sure did. Let him out, Bo."

Bo opened his own door then, and a big, brown blur leaped over the seat onto his lap, then sprang onto the driveway.

Everyone stared. The dog wagged his tail. His coat was perfectly trimmed and brushed. In fact, he looked cream-rinsed and combed. A large bow sat lopsided around his neck.

"Mooch?"

"Mooch?"

"Nooo."

The dog stopped wagging his tail and hung his head in shame.

Then Chelsea pulled a candy bar out of her purse and began to unwrap it.

"Woof! Woof!"

Chelsea tossed it to him.

He caught it with a perfectly timed snap of the jaw.

"Mooch!" everyone said.

"What did they do to you, old boy?" asked Connor. "It must have been thorough and brutal. I wonder if they could do it to me."

"You? You're hopeless," said Chelsea, grabbing a fistful of Connor's red hair.

"So, you're saying that I shouldn't even try to make an appointment at Poodle Parlor, Dee Dee's Dogorama, Beastly Best—Canine Cutie?"

They were both laughing. At last, thought Kate.

"I'm taking this ribbon off," Bo told Grace. "The lady said that since you were paying for it, we had to leave it on and that we couldn't let Mooch out to play in the dirt until you saw him."

"Why did you do this?" Kate asked. "Did Mooch look that bad?"

"Not just looked, smelled," Grace replied. "Though David has warned me, he'll start smelling again soon enough. He better like it at Animal Artistes. He has a weekly appointment, which he has to make if he intends to stay in my room."

"He can stay in my room," Kate offered. "I'm used to sleeping with him."

"So am I," said Grace.

Their eyes met and there was an uncomfortable silence.

"Well," said Connor, "I think I'll start unpacking. Can I have your keys, Kate? While we're unloading our apartment, we're bound to come across that tiny little suitcase you brought. Chels or I will bring it over. Come on, beautiful. No! No! Not you, Mooch."

After Connor and Chelsea had gone off to their new apartment, Bo and Mooch headed toward the beach and Marta to the clinic. She was picking up a late shift until all the personnel were back in place. David said he had to go—he had a flying lesson to give. Handing Grace her car keys, he climbed onto his motorcycle. The surprise on Grace's face told Kate that a lesson wasn't really on the schedule; he was making an excuse to leave. To leave Kate and Grace alone.

FIVE

"So, how are you doing?" Grace asked.

"Fine," said Kate. She tried to sound warmer, friendlier, but at the sight of Mooch—now, apparently, Grace's Mooch—she had gone ice cold inside. "Thanks again for asking me down here."

Grace shrugged. "It helps me as much as you."

"I'm sorry about your mother."

Grace's only response was a nod.

"So," Kate said, "while I'm waiting to get my things, I think I'll take a peek at the ocean. I haven't seen it for a long time."

"Of course."

Kate had hoped Grace would leave her then, but instead she led the way on the narrow path of boards that skirted the house. Kate had no choice but to follow.

Last year she had rushed to the sea, hurtling herself across the boardwalk, over the burning sand, and into the freezing May water, clothes and all. Now, though the open beach lay before her, she found herself veering away from it. She moved toward the boardwalk, climbed up its two steps, and leaned on the railing, looking out at the sea. "It looks just the same."

"It is the same," Grace said.

"Kind of calm today."

"Incredible, isn't it." It was a statement, not a question. "Calm and blue, with all those little ruffle waves."

Kate was conscious of Grace studying her. She kept her eyes on the ocean.

"Would you rather see it wild and black, Kate, so it all makes some sense? I, for one, find it hard to wave an angry fist at an ocean that babies can play in."

"I'm not angry," said Kate.

"Oh."

"And I'd like to be alone."

"Well, at least you know what you want," Grace said with a grim smile. "I can't seem to decide. One moment I'm telling people to leave me alone. The next I'm wandering about in my own house, thinking I'll go crazy if I don't have another body there. Back and forth I go. Leave me alone! Come quickly!"

Kate thought about Tosh and felt a little guilty.

"But today, right now, at this moment, I know. I need to be with you."

62

Kate turned sharply. Apparently Grace didn't care about Kate's needs.

"You're not angry, are you?" Grace asked slyly. "You're not angry at me?"

"No," Kate replied firmly. "I just said I wasn't. Why should I be? I'd like to walk."

"I could use some exercise too," Grace said.

They started down the boardwalk together, Kate keeping her eyes straight ahead, Grace looking at the string of buildings they passed: clapboard apartment houses, old hotels with squadrons of empty rockers, and motels with decks sprouting plastic palm trees. The farther south they got, the tackier it got. Restaurants with red-glass windows and colonial waitresses, shops that sold abalone ashtrays and obscene T-shirts, the Wild West miniature golf next to the Polynesian Wonder course, food stands and their monuments—gigantic plastic lemons, tacos, and crabs—dotted the way.

That afternoon Grace could walk without looking where she was going. By the evening, the boardwalk would be jammed. When the girls passed The Claw, one of the nicest and most romantic restaurants in town, Kate glanced over.

"Looks good, doesn't it?" Grace remarked. "It got a new face this winter. . . . You did too, by the way."

Kate looked straight ahead again and quickened her pace.

"I didn't think you could get much more intense, but you did," Grace observed.

Kate's fingers balled into fists; then she forced herself to uncoil them and relax.

"It's all right to be angry," Grace added.

"I am not angry," said Kate.

"He died loving you, you know?"

"I guess that's why he stopped writing," said Kate.

"Men are lousy writers. That's just their nature. He may have mailed only one or two letters, but he kept all of yours," she said. "Do you want them back?"

"You have them?"

"Yes. Do you want them?"

"No," Kate replied. "That part of my life is over."

"Okay. Can I read them?"

"You bitch!" cried Kate. "You bitch!"

"Now, that's more like it," said Grace, her eyes glinting.

"You're trying to making me angry."

"I didn't have to work very hard."

"You bitch!"

"Do you think I want to be the only one walking around furious? Be glad you got only *one* person to be mad at for dying on you."

"What I want to know," Kate said, "is if there wasn't a way you could have—" She checked herself.

"Could have saved him?" Grace finished the sentence. "Do you want to hear the story again? Or were you just asking that to let me know you blame me?"

"I don't blame you. I don't! It's irrational, I know it—Tosh told me so. Besides, I spend most of my time blaming myself. I can't help wondering, what if *I* had decided to go with him?"

"So *you* could have saved him?" Grace asked sarcastically. "I've tried that line on myself a number of times: 'Kate's a swimmer. If Kate had been with him, she would have leaped in and saved him. Against all odds, our heroine Kate would have dragged him up out of the depths of the sea.'"

They stared at each other, their eyes glistening, hot and full of tears.

"It's all right to cry, too," Grace said. "Or so David tells me."

Kate turned away. She didn't like this new Grace, didn't trust a Grace who was reaching out.

"Kate, listen to me. Listen! We both have to let ourselves get angry, and let ourselves get over it, and over him. We have to. If we won't do it for the good of ourselves, then for the others we love—David and Bo and . . . Tosh?"

Kate swallowed. Her throat felt dry and tight. "I guess so," she said at last. "I know so. That's the way Justin would have wanted it."

Grace nodded. "What would Justin say if he

65

saw the two of us, beautiful women both, walking down the boardwalk, getting all wound up and teary over the memory of him?"

For a moment they were silent; then they both said at the same time, *"He'd love it!"*

They laughed and, maybe because they had wanted so much to cry and had held back, laughed wildly, and staggered down the boardwalk, colliding into each other. For a moment they linked arms.

"Whew!" said Grace. "It's bad enough that we almost bonded last summer. Now look at us."

Kate pulled her arm away, still laughing. "Hey, what did you do to your elbow?"

"Never mind that," Grace said. "Tell me about this new guy. Chelsea dropped a few hints when I talked to her. Who's this Tosh?"

"Tosh," Kate said, then dug into her pocket. "Kleenex?"

"Thanks. Now tell me."

"He's smart. Kind. Good-looking. Mature."

"Well, you know how I feel about older men," Grace interjected.

"I'm glad you're still with David."

"Me too. But don't sidetrack. Tosh?"

"He knows I need time. He really understands. He was really great about me coming down here for the summer."

"Really? I never trust a man who is really great and really understanding about things. But

that's just Grace the cynic speaking. In any case, it is definitely good for you to be here this summer, and it would be even better if you dated around a bit. I'm giving Marta some encouragement too. We just talked about it."

Kate looked at Grace, cocking her head sideways. "What is this, Grace the mother hen?"

"I'd like my roost to be a happy one."

Kate just shook her head and laughed.

"Hey, girls, laughing girls!" a man called to them. He was standing inside the door of Iguana Saloon. "Wet T-shirt contest, Memorial Day. We'll pack 'em in, girls, we'll pack 'em in."

"So," said Grace, "let the madness begin."

Marta banged through the swinging doors. "I want Landon in Room Two. Call Dr. Weinstein and let him know we got a bleeder. Where's the man who keeps throwing up?"

"In the bathroom throwing up," said Ming. "Slow down, Marta. You're laying tire tracks."

She grinned up at her comrade-in-arms. "Where did all these people come from?"

"Somewhere on the other side of the bridge," Ming replied, running his hand through dark, bristly hair. "Let's send them back."

"Agreed," she said. "Is Judy a help to you?"

He looked over at the new girl, a sixteen-year-old with a headful of short blond curls and a bouncy kind of walk. "How'd she get the job?"

he asked. "One of her parents a doctor?"

"That bad?" said Marta.

Ming grimaced.

"Well, we just have to get through this crazy weekend; then things will settle down and I'll have time to train her."

"I guess if anyone can, you can," he said doubtfully, then pushed an empty wheelchair past her, glancing at the next name on his list. "Mr. Landon?"

Marta moved toward the desk where Judy was taking down a patient's history.

"You're kidding!" Judy exclaimed at the older woman. "You're kidding! Three transfusions! Lordy-lord! Aren't you afraid you got AIDS?"

Marta rolled swiftly beside Judy.

"Oh, hi!" Judy said cheerfully.

Her patient was looking white as a ghost.

"Hello, Mrs. . . . . McPhail," Marta said quietly, leaning to look at her chart. "What seems to be the trouble?"

The old woman shook as she told Marta how she had smashed her finger in the car door. She had wrapped it up and gone to bed because she hated hospitals, just hated them, they made her so nervous. . . .

Ten minutes later, when Marta had brought Mrs. McPhail's blood pressure down from stroke range, she pulled Judy aside in the hallway.

"Judy, when you are interviewing a patient,

you are not to remark upon what the patient tells you. You simply write it down. Do not, I repeat, do not discuss with the patient his or her medical history. Leave that to the doctor, okay?"

"Okay," she replied with a bright smile.

"Now, would you give this to Mr. Landon for his urine specimen? Here are the instructions."

The girl's eyes opened wide.

Marta gazed back at her, puzzled for a moment, then said, "*He* does it. Himself. The instructions are for him."

"Phew!" said Judy. "I wasn't quite ready for that. You know, I'm new."

"I know," said Marta. "It is your job," she added, "to pick up the specimen afterward. Make sure it has its label with the patient's name before you set it in the lab tray."

Judy went bobbing off, and Marta returned to Cubicle 4. She chatted up a six-year-old, discussed with him the possibility of doing wheelies in her chair, and at a discreet moment slipped a needle in his arm. The same techniques wouldn't work with the forty-six-year-old in the next room. "This will hurt like hell," she said with a wicked grin. The man laughed and she got him right then.

Then it was back to the waiting room. Two A.M. and every seat filled, she observed. In one night, a night they were short of doctors, how could so many people hack themselves with kitchen knives, step on nails, fall off skateboards, and eat bad imperial crab?

Her eyes swept the crowded room, then stopped. Him. The guy on the boardwalk. Obviously their stars were crossed tonight.

He hadn't seen her yet. He was sitting, chatting quietly to the old man next to him, Mr. DiPaola, one of the clinic's most frequent—and healthy—visitors.

In spite of herself, Marta picked up the last chart to be set in the bin. Ming had filled it out. "The usual" he wrote, but he had written in the name of the one who brought Mr. DiPaola. The old man always liked them to do that. Dominic Velasquez. She repeated the name to herself.

Dominic was now hunched over in his chair, staring at his feet. The old man was holding his hand. Then he tapped Dominic on the arm and said something to him. Dominic looked up, straight across the room and into Marta's face. He visibly paled, as he had earlier that day.

What is it with him? Marta thought. She didn't need this kind of crap tonight.

What is it with *you*, Marta? she chided herself. Checking out a guy's name on a patient chart. How professional!

She wheeled around so fast, she nearly bulldozed Ming and had to make a sharp cut to the right.

"You know, the Harlem Globetrotters could use someone like you," he said.

She grunted and zipped through the doors, just in time to hear Judy say, "Uh-oh!"

"What?" said Marta.

"Uh, remember when you told me to get Mr. Landon's urine?"

"Five minutes ago," said Marta.

"Well, after that, Ming asked me to get Mrs. Smith's."

Marta guessed what was coming next.

"Uh, do you think maybe hers would be a little warmer and therefore we—"

"This clinic doesn't operate in nearly so scientific a way," Marta said sarcastically. "If we don't label samples, we get new ones. Get them."

Two minutes later Judy was back.

"He says he can't. She says she'll try, but she's not sure." Marta rolled over to the refrigerator. She pulled out four bottles of juice. "Tell them to drink up," she said. "Tell them they *will*."

Sighing, she went back out to the waiting room. Her eyes swept one side, then the other, leaving a hole where Dominic sat. But old Mr. DiPaola caught her eye. Then he remembered to clutch his side for a dramatic moment. She nodded to him.

"A long wait tonight, yes, Marta?" he called to her, not so feebly.

"Yes, Mr. DiPaola," she called back. "You just rest easy."

He gestured to her to come over.

"This is Marta," the old man said when she was close. He touched her name tag, which gave only her first name. "Not Miss Marta, just Marta."

She smiled a little at the old man, then forced herself to look from him to Dominic. Dominic was already staring at her. Looking into his eyes was like looking into endless night, gazing into the black sky between stars. She felt held by some kind of dark gravity. A girl could get lost in those eyes, she thought, and pulled away her own.

"Are you doing all right?" she asked Mr. DiPaola. "Should I—"

He made little calming motions with his hands, then patted both her and Dominic on the leg. "Everything's all right, under control," he said. "You'll get to me all in good time. I'm a patient man, you know."

She knew. She wished he would complain of chest pains or something, so she had a valid reason to rush him ahead of others, and rush Dominic out of there. She felt as if every professional nerve of her body had been tested tonight. But that was before she heard the "Aah!" and thud on the floor behind her.

She spun around. A night fisherman was bleeding all over their tiles. A nasty hook wound—but he was standing upright. Whom should she tend to first, him or the prostrate Judy?

Ming took the fisherman. "I know how to deal with *these* types," he said meaningfully.

Marta brought Judy around, then helped her through the swinging doors, steering her into a vacated cubicle. When the girl's color returned, Marta did the kindest thing she could think of. She told her to go home, get a few hours of sleep, and call Grace between eight and nine A.M. "There's nothing like a job on the beach. You get fresh air, guys to look at, and a free umbrella to sit under," she added, and went on to the next patient.

At three forty A.M. she was whizzing through the waiting room. Three seats were now empty. We're making progress, Marta thought. I've got things under control.

"Uh, Miss Salgado?" Dominic called.

Almost, she thought.

"Miss Salgado?" He sounded panicky.

"Mr. Velasquez," she said, turning toward him. She remembered too late that the old man hadn't introduced Dominic by name, but Dominic didn't seem to wonder how she knew it.

"What's wrong with him?" he asked.

Marta glanced at Mr. DiPaola. "I'm not a doctor, but I'd say he's tired. And he's got a wicked snore." She started off.

"But you don't understand!" Dominic cried. "He could be seriously injured. You can't keep

73

him waiting like this, waiting all night. He could be bleeding internally. He could have a concussion. I didn't want to bring him in without a stretcher. I told him, something could—could snap and he could be paralyzed for the rest of his life." As soon as he said it, he look as if he wished he hadn't.

"Really," said Marta. "Then by all means, get that chair from over there and bring him in."

Dominic obeyed humbly, following her through the doors to Cubicle 3.

"Mr. DiPaola. Wake up, Mr. DiPaola," Marta said, pulling the striped curtain around the three of them.

"Huh? Huh? Oh, Marta."

"Time to treat you and let you go home. Where did you get hit this time?"

"My arm. And my ribs. Definitely my ribs."

Marta nodded, then got out an alcohol pad. She gently lifted the man's shirt and wiped the spot he pointed to. It was soft and white as a baby's skin. Then she got out a second pad and wiped another unbruised spot on his arm.

She put her hand against his forehead.

"I might have a temperature," he said.

"A temperature!" said Dominic. "From being hit by a car?"

And then it dawned on him. Poor sucker, she thought. He thought he had really struck the man. He wasn't the first. The old man deserved an Oscar.

Dominic's eyes flashed black. This is trouble, she thought.

She grabbed Dominic by the arm and dragged him out of the cubicle, down the hall so Mr. DiPaola wouldn't hear them.

"What the hell!" he hissed. "What the hell, that old man."

She couldn't help grinning. She covered her mouth with her hand, but she knew her eyes were giving her away. She threw back her head and laughed—laughed and laughed. She wished Grace were here to see his expression.

His eyes were on her, on the long neck and the black hair that was twisting free of its butterfly clamp.

She choked herself into silence, and he turned away.

"Sorry," she said, but a giggle broke through.

He turned back, then dropped down into an easy crouch. He was lower than her now, looking up into her face. "So." There was the slightest smile on his lips. "I've been duped."

"Big time!" she said, then added, "He's a very lonely old man. Don't yell at him. People have, but to what effect? You can't yell away someone's loneliness. You can't yell away their pain. Right now he's ready to go home, quite content. He got to sit with someone for two hours and have his hand patted."

"*He* patted mine," said Dominic.

"It comes out just the same," she replied.

"Does it?" He reached then, and laid his hand on top of hers.

Marta let it stay there for a moment, then slipped hers out from under.

For the rest of the night, she found herself wondering. What did that gesture mean? Was he feeling some sympathy for her, or was he the one seeking comfort?

SIX

Kate pulled the sweatshirt over her head and peeled off her pants. She was all goose bumps. At six A.M. on a gray day with wind blowing out of the north at 12 knots, air temp 65, and the ocean an unwelcoming 58 degrees, everyone had goose bumps—except Marta's father.

It was possible that Luis Salgado, who had arrived wearing his red trunks, nothing else, had a different sort of blood pumping through him. Maybe the day the great white took a chomp out of him—the story behind his scar was just about legend now—a dose of shark had gotten mixed in. Luis's prey was any member of the beach patrol who wasn't doing the job 150 percent. And he could pick up their scent three guard stands away.

Kate watched him as he talked with one of his lieutenants, one of the lifeguards he relied upon most. If Justin were alive, Luis would be conversing with him. If Justin were alive—

"Name, please," said another of Luis's lieutenants.

"Quinn, Kate."

"Fifty-two," he said, handing her a bathing cap with the number marked on it. A second guard grabbed her arm and branded her with a thick black grease pencil.

Now, Kate thought grimly, when they drag me out of the surf, limp as seaweed, someone will still be able to identify me.

The lifeguard trials were notoriously grinding. But that hadn't stopped sixty-some people from showing up, hoping to win the last ten slots on the force. The rest of the patrol had been hired during the early weeks of May.

Most of the candidates were guys. Spotting three girls at the other edge of the crowd, Kate was tempted to join them. But it seemed weak somehow for the females to huddle together. Kate stayed where she was, close to the water. The cold, salty spray blowing off the water stung her skin. Kate curled her toes into sand that was still soaked and covered with broken shells. Bending over at the waist, she began doing warm-up stretches.

"Sixty trying out," said the guy next to her. He too was hanging upside down. "Know what that means? Five out of six will be left wrapping taffy at Dilly's."

"Those are the breaks," said Kate.

"Wonder what the quota is for women?" he added.

Kate straightened up quickly, and a moment later he righted himself.

"Luis doesn't think that way," she told him, then began twisting from side to side.

"Luis, is it? Do you know Mr. Salgado?" He waited till her eyes were on him, then flexed his muscles and checked out her reaction. His hair looked chlorine gold. No doubt, all the girls who supported the college swim team found him impressive.

The boy next to him had the same color hair, but a much slighter build. He probably lifeguarded at a health club, Kate thought. "Wish *I* knew him," the health-club type said.

"It doesn't matter," replied Kate. "We all look the same in these bathing caps."

Mr. Swimteam eyed her up and down, letting his eyes stop where he pleased. "If you want to guard, you're going to have to be a lot more observant than that."

She didn't respond.

"Me, I don't miss a thing." He turned to the health-club guy. "Check out those flotation devices over there."

In spite of herself, Kate glanced back at the three girls she had noticed before. Since some of the candidates had started into the water, she had a clear view of one of the girls. Good grief! Dolly Parton in a Speedo!

A whistle blew, signaling five minutes till the start of the first trial. Kate made a running plunge into the water.

Agh! Merciless, briny cold. But that was the least of it. There was a powerful current running south. The course was set so they'd be swimming north. Good. She had prepared all winter for this, and she was hungry for a hard swim. She loved the way the ocean scoured her body. She loved how it allowed her to think of nothing but the most elemental things: motion, breathing, light, dark, air. Survival. She swam and swam, exhilarated.

The candidates, having finished their warm-up, were called out of the ocean, and the three timed trials were explained. The swimmers would compete in packs of twenty. In the first trial, called Run-Swim-Run, they had to dash 150 yards up the beach, then swim 150 yards out to a buoy. Rounding the buoy, they'd swim another 150 yards north to a second buoy, then head back to the beach for a final 150-yard sprint.

"And then, untimely death."

Kate spun around. "Connor!"

"Shall we bury you at sea, Kate, tolling ship bells all the way, or would you like to be interred in your family plot? We could put you in *my* family plot—you said you've always wanted to visit Ireland."

"Connor, what are you doing here?"

"I've come to cheer you on, dear Kate."

She looked at him with disbelief. It was five hours before his natural rising time.

"All right, maybe I had other reasons," he admitted. "Like paying the rent and convincing my bride I can handle a most respectable job. I'm covering this for 'Beach Babble.'"

"'Beach Babble'?"

"Keep your voice down," he said. "I don't want Chlorine-Head to find me again."

Kate followed Connor's eyes over to the larger of the two guys with whom she had been talking.

"He's way too anxious to give quotes," Connor told her. "Speaking of which, I could use some from you. You know—how does it feel, other than cold? What are your hopes, your dreams, et cetera?"

"I take it 'Beach Babble' is the name of an article for the *Gazette*."

"The name of a column," replied Connor. "I'm trying to get it changed, but the editor thinks it's cute. I'll probably end up changing my own name instead. So, are you nervous?"

"You're the one who's chattering," she said.

"You'll do fine. Chelsea prayed for you last night."

Kate smiled a little and nodded. She watched the first twenty candidates charge down the beach.

"She prayed to Justin."

"What?" Recovering herself, she said, "How is she so certain about which place he went to?"

Connor gave a crooked grin and shrugged. "Saint Justin. Patron of Lifeguards and the Lost at Sea. It has a ring to it. I can see him now, standing in a stained-glass window."

"In his little red trunks," said Kate.

"Mmm. He'll be a very popular saint," Connor mused. "Imagine all the ladies looking devoutly up at him—I'm saying all the wrong things, aren't I, Kate?"

She watched the second group of candidates line up for their trial. "It doesn't really matter."

"It matters to me. I want to see you get this job. And when you do," he added, "you wouldn't mind me making up some interesting quotes, just to make it a touch more dramatic?"

"Of course not. And when we get to the Surf Rescue trial, you wouldn't mind me dragging you into the waves, instead of the red torpedo? Your hair's long enough for a rope."

"Uh, I think I'll go look for Chlorine-Head," he said. "Godspeed, Kate."

He slipped away and Kate started pacing. It was a relief to be called to the starting line.

At the sound of the gun, she took off. Her face was taut with concentration, and she had to order herself to relax. She focused on what her body was doing, breathing evenly, extending her legs, pushing against the sand. She kept herself toward the front of the pack without setting the pace.

When she hit the water, the heat in her skin exploded out of her. For a moment she felt confused, as if she couldn't read the turbulent water with the pack of bodies moving around her. She misjudged a wave and lost time. Her body felt as if it were pulling back on her. She started swimming hard, but now she was bringing up the rear.

Still, she kept her head and, rounding the buoy, swam in the wake of the swimmer just ahead of her, darting out and around him at the last moment. She pursued each swimmer in turn, passing three, four, five, six of her competitors. Now she was in the middle of the pack, rounding the second buoy.

She didn't want to use her last spurt of energy, not this soon, not with a group this fast. But she could feel the drag and knew a wave was building behind her, building quickly. She had to choose. With a fierce kick, Kate gave it her all.

Just when she thought she had missed the wave, she felt its lift and rush. She went flying toward shore, landing ten meters ahead of everyone else. She ran the next 150 yards, her legs almost numb and her lungs burning. She crossed the line first, a half step in front of Chlorine-Head.

Kate wanted to look cool, self-assured, and unconcerned, but she couldn't help it: as soon as she crossed the line, she looked over at Luis. He didn't seem to notice her. Doesn't matter, she said to herself. Her time and placement were recorded.

She sat down dutifully with the others who, between trials, were taking the written exam. She glanced down the sheet she was dripping on: surf characteristics, decision making, first aid. Well, she had come prepared for this.

Her body was just starting to cool down when she was called up for the Surf Rescue. She warmed up quickly and kept herself warm afterward. But her body began to rebel when the Run-Paddle-Run was announced.

Kate did well in both trials; still, when only one out of six would make it, was it well enough?

She watched with everyone else as Luis conferred with his lieutenants. After two and a half hours of trials and tension, most of the candidates were sitting. A few were stretched out on their backs. Then it was announced that there would be one more Run-Swim-Run. This time they'd race as a whole pack.

"You can't tell me he hasn't made up his mind!" snapped a redhead.

The black guy next to him agreed. "He's just doing this to see how far he can push us."

"Get used to it," said the lieutenant who had overheard them.

Kate got up without a word. She stretched, then found a spot in the pack. When the gun went off, so did she. But she was on automatic pilot now. She swam with energy she didn't know she had. Her body seemed severed from her brain. She could have been a chicken with her head chopped off, her body still moving, not knowing it was dead.

At last the trial was over. Bodies swayed beyond the finish line. Kate flopped down on the beach and pulled on her sweats. Connor came over and plunked down beside her.

"I'd put my arm around you," he said, "but I don't want you to look anything less than macho."

"Appreciate it, Connor."

"Quinn," Luis called. "Quinn!"

"Here," she said, then stood up, Connor giving her the extra shove she needed to make it all the way.

Luis walked over to her, staring down at his clipboard. "I just want to know," he said, "why you doing this?"

"Why?" she repeated vaguely.

"Why," said Luis. "Smart girl like you should know what 'why' means."

Kate was aware of the silence around her, aware of all the guys staring at her, of the curiosity on the lieutenants' faces and the interest of Connor, with his pad out and pencil poised. A wave of anger washed over her. Luis hadn't questioned any of the male candidates.

"Because I, like Miss America, want to save the world?" she said sweetly.

"Or Justin," said Luis.

"Justin's dead."

Luis snorted. "He was a damn good lifeguard, one of the best I ever had. He could have taught you a few things," he said, then frowned down at his clipboard.

"He did teach me one thing."

"What's that?" asked Luis, without looking up.

"That even one of the best can make mistakes. And those who are lucky enough to survive must learn from them."

"Is that so." He walked away from her then. When he was out of sight, she collapsed on the sand again.

"By God, you're good, Kate," said Connor. "I'm not going to have to make anything up."

She nodded mutely and gazed out at the gray and restless sea.

"Okay, folks," said one of the lieutenants. "Listen up."

Out of the corner of her eye Kate saw Luis heading toward his truck, as if he had nothing to do with all the chilly, sweating people on the beach. His lieutenant said, "We thank you all for coming. Here's the list of new guards. Listen up, because I'm not going to repeat it. Ursbrook.

Maisel. Danner. Whitehead. Krasnansky. Smith. Wagner. Petracek. Helldorfer. And Quinn."

Quinn.

Kate turned to Connor. "You can put your arm around me now."

SEVEN

"Almost done, Bo," Grace said, dusting the sand off her hands and slipping the padlock on the last of the big wooden crates where the umbrellas and surf mats were stored. People trudged past her, carrying coolers and boom boxes, buckets and kites. Many of the beachgoers were wearing sweat suits, so it looked like a parade of colorful teddy bears. On such a cool, sunless day, this stand was the only one that had made any real money.

That Judy girl was good!

Bo had come with Grace to help her close down the stands. She had asked him to learn the procedure so he could cover for her. As usual these days, he traveled by skateboard.

"Okay," Grace said, picking up the strongbox with the money in it, "you're my armed guard, Bo. Bo?"

She turned to survey the crowd on the board-walk, then heard the piercing scream of a girl, followed by a heavy metallic sound and an "Oh, shi-oot!" that belonged to Bo.

Grace rushed up the wooden steps, the heavy box banging against her leg. Bo, a girl, a skateboard, a trash can, and a fine mess of scabby-looking pizza lay in the middle of the boardwalk.

Bo looked bewildered. The girl was holding her eye. She let out another shrill sound. Grace ran forward, afraid the pedestrian was seriously hurt. She pulled the girl's hand away from her face. There was a cut by the edge of her eye-brow, but it was less than an inch long and superficial.

The girl glared up at her.

"She's going to live," Grace assured Bo.

"You stupid butthead," the girl said. "You could have killed me. Why didn't you look where you were going?"

"Why didn't I? Why didn't *you*? She jumped down in front of me, Grace," Bo said. He pointed to the boardwalk railing.

"You're lying," the girl cried, and Grace noticed the long Southern drawl in her voice. "Why, I could sue you! I could sue you for every-thing you're worth."

"Are we getting just a bit dramatic?" Grace asked.

The girl tilted her head back to look at Grace.

Grace knew that butt-out-bitch look quite well. She had used it countless times in her own life, and she almost laughed at her mirror image. "What's your name?" she asked.

The girl lowered her chin a little, but continued to stare hard at Grace. Her short hair was bleached blond and wispy, her eyes were huge and brown.

"Are you staying around here?" Grace inquired.

The girl simply blinked.

"Get me some napkins from that stand, Bo," Grace said quietly. "And a glass of ice water."

He hurried off.

"What's your name?" Grace asked again, feeling her patience draining away.

"What's it to you?"

"Mud," said Grace, "but I was wondering what your friends call you."

"Roan."

"Roan what?"

"Just Roan."

"How are old you, Just Roan?"

The girl fidgeted. "Sixteen."

"I'd say fifteen at the most," said Grace. "Thanks, Bo. She began to dab the wound with the wet napkins. The girl flinched a little, but kept her face toward Grace.

"In addition to this cut, you're going to have a shiner," Grace told her.

"It won't be the first," Roan replied.

"Tough, are we? That's why we got that little rose tattooed on our ankle?"

"Why do you keep saying *we*?"

"Who knows," said Grace, smiling wryly. "My mother used to. Now I'm doing it. Where are you staying?"

"None of your business."

"It *is* my business. If you're suing my brother, our lawyer will want your address. You are suing, aren't you? I love a good fight."

"Give me a break," said the girl, pulling herself up. She looked at Bo, but jerked her head toward Grace. "You got to live with her? I feel sorry for you."

"Living with Grace is cool," said Bo.

"Beats living under the boardwalk," Grace added.

Roan turned away quickly. Then she faced Grace again and gave her the finger.

Bingo, thought Grace. "The O.C. clinic is not far from here," she said. "I'll drive you there. The cut isn't too bad, but that trash can is rusty. You should have a tetanus shot."

"You telling me what to do?"

"You don't have to use your real name," Grace continued. "I'll sign for you if permission is needed. And I'll pay."

The girl smiled with one side of her mouth, then gave Grace the finger a second time.

"That's getting a little old," said Grace. "Don't you have another favorite expression?"

"Screw you," the girl replied, and walked away.

Grace watched her for a half a block, then turned to Bo. "Well, that's enough Mother Teresa for one day. Let's hit the road."

But when she got in her BMW and started easing her way out of the side street, all she could think about was that kid. Each red light she stopped at, each blond girl she glimpsed, she checked out twice. Any kid who acted that angry and tough was very angry—and anything but tough inside, Grace knew. Sighing, she turned the car around.

"What are you doing, Gracie?"

"Making a fool of myself," she said.

She drove back to Tenth Street, where the accident had taken place, pulling all the way up into the no-parking spot close to the boardwalk.

There she was. Somehow Grace had guessed that she would wander back. Lost people always do hang around the same spot.

Roan had her back to them. She was talking to two older guys. Grace saw one of them reach in his pocket and hand her some money.

When the guys had walked on, she called out, "Roan! Just Roan!"

The girl swung around.

"Come on," said Grace.

"Leave me alone."

Grace pointed to her car. "Get in!"

Roan looked as if she were about to shoot up the finger again.

"Uh, miss, excuse me. You're in a no-parking, no-stopping, no-standing zone."

Grace turned around to look at the cop, who was as young as she and wearing an expression that said: Please leave, because I don't know what to do next. But Grace was thinking fast, and she knew what to do.

"Officer," she said loudly, "if I know of someone, a minor, who has run away from home, should I report her to you or should I call the station?" Out of the corner of her eye she saw Roan wanting to bolt, but afraid to miss what was being said. "I can give a *very* accurate description," she added.

Roan started to make a face, then caught herself. Grace smiled: she really was just a kid.

"Call the station. In a town like this, they're used to handling that kind of thing. Though, of course, I could take the information down now, if you like, I suppose. I have time, if you have time, I suppose." He fumbled for a pencil.

"Do we have time, Roan? Or should we go to the clinic first?"

Roan glared at her. Then she thumped down the boardwalk ramp and climbed into the back of the car.

Grace made no attempt at conversation on

94

the way over. Bo's eyes were wide and wary.

They registered her as Roan Caywood, and Ming took her back to clean her wound and give her a shot. Grace started flipping through a magazine, ignoring the sullen expression on Bo's face. If she'd given him his way, they'd be paying for Roan and cutting out before the girl was returned to them.

A few minutes after Roan went in, Marta came out.

"Grace, what are you doing here?"

"Playing mommy. How about you?"

"Playing doctor."

"Oh, well, given our years of training, I can't think of two more qualified people."

"What's wrong, Bo?" Marta asked.

"It's not me."

Marta turned to Grace, her eyes questioning.

"Perhaps you saw the patient, or heard her. That nice little girl Ming took back with him a few minutes ago."

"Oh, *that* one," said Marta.

"She's not giving you any trouble, is she? She has the sweetest way of giving you the finger."

Marta laughed. "Where did you find her?"

"On the boardwalk," Grace replied. "We have Bo to thank for that."

"And we have Grace to thank for offering her a place to stay!" said Bo.

"You didn't!" said Marta. "You did?"

"Not yet. At the moment, we're not speaking. But before I drop her off again, I will."

Marta bit her lip. Bo shook his head in disbelief.

"I have to," Grace said. "She reminds me of someone I know."

"Who?" Marta asked curiously.

"None of your business," Grace said, then laughed. "Don't worry. I know this kid. She'll say no to the offer. She *lives* to say no."

"Kate, this is Roan," said Grace. "She'll be staying with us for a bit."

Kate looked up from a countertop spread with orientation materials. She noted the worn clothes and the bruise, growing like a purple-and-yellow pansy around the girl's eye. She was curious, but decided not to ask what had happened.

"That's nice," she said. "How long are you staying?"

Roan shrugged.

"As long as she can stand the rules," said Grace.

"What rules?" Kate asked, then bit her tongue.

Roan gave a sarcastic smile. "The rules she made up especially for me."

"Well," said Kate. "Welcome. The more the merrier!"

"I'm glad to hear you say that."

Kate jumped at the voice.

Grace laughed. "He was in the driveway when we arrived. He says his name is Tosh. So I guess he is that *really* understanding guy, huh?"

Kate opened her mouth, but no words came out. Tosh stood in the doorway with his head cocked, smiling at her. She tried to smile back, but her face felt stiff.

Tosh's look of amusement faded. "You don't look very happy to see me," he said.

"You're—you're supposed to be in Florida."

He gave a little shrug and smiled again. "I was on my way there and ran into a couple of states in between, like this one."

"Why didn't you call?" Kate asked.

"I wanted to surprise you," Tosh told her.

"Well, you did." Kate stood up but didn't move toward him. "Uh, welcome to Ocean City."

"Come on, Roan." Grace took her by the arm. "Let me show you your room. It's downstairs with Marta's."

"And where is Frosty's?" Kate heard Roan ask as she and Grace headed toward the stairs.

"I didn't mean to be cold, Tosh. I just wasn't expecting you," Kate tried to explain.

"You were expecting someone else?"

"No, no," she stammered.

"You're busy with something, I can see." He glanced down at a paper, Beach Patrol Rules & Regulations. "You did it. Kate, you did it! Congratulations!" His arms opened wide, and the next moment Kate was wrapped in them.

"I did it," she said, her face against his neck.

He kissed her softly, briefly, then held her back a little. "Look at those shining eyes," he said.

She grinned at him

"So, when do I get to throw down my towel, cast in my lot with all the muscle-bound hunks arranging themselves around your lifeguard chair? I wonder how many of them will pretend to drown the first day."

"Oh, come on," said Kate.

"Hmmm?" He pulled her close again. Very close. His hands traveled over her. She held still, not wanting to reject him but wishing he'd let her go.

"So you have reading to do," he said at last.

"Yes," she answered with relief.

"Shall we have dinner first? Driving in, I passed a restaurant I would love to take you to. The Hurricane Lamp, do you know it? It looked very romantic. Tables on the bay."

It was very romantic, lit solely by candles in hurricane globes and having a long deck over-looking the water.

"I've already eaten," she said, hoping he wouldn't look around the corner and see the half bowl of cereal in the sink. She just couldn't go and hold hands with Tosh by the bay. She hadn't ventured back there yet, though on this narrow island the bay lay only a few blocks west of the ocean. The bay belonged to Justin. It was where he had dreamed, where they had swum out at night, where—

She cut off these thoughts. "What can I fix you for dinner?" she said, moving into the kitchen area, opening the refrigerator.

"You're sure you don't want to go, not even for dessert?"

"I'm sorry. I really do have a lot of reading to do."

He nodded.

They fixed omelets together, mixing together an odd assortment of leftovers. Tosh didn't comment on the fact that she was suddenly hungry again. He started teasing, suggesting all the opening lines that she'd hear from guys he was certain would encircle her guard chair. Kate smiled, then giggled, then laughed out loud.

Roan came back in, and Tosh turned his sense of humor on her, bad puns and all. When he made a joke about Roan's black eye, Kate was half afraid the girl would swing at him. But she smiled a little, just enough to egg Tosh on. Grace joined them and more omelets were made. Then Bo came in with Mooch, who was always happy to be in the breakfast room.

"This is Mooch?" Tosh said with surprise. "That's not how I pictured him."

"He's been to rehab," Grace replied.

Not long after, Marta arrived.

Tosh leaped up from his seat and began mixing more stuff in the frying pan.

He loves this, thought Kate. It's as if he's in the classroom again, talking and entertaining everyone.

"I was making this omelet for Mooch," he told Marta, "but you can have it. You don't mind liver bits, do you?"

"I guess they're high in iron," she said.

When everyone had finished, Tosh offered to clean up. "After all, you have to work tomorrow. I'm just going to lie on the beach all day with nothing more to do than roll over from time to time." He turned to Roan. "How about you?" he asked. "If you're not working, I'm afraid we'll have to be scullery maids together."

"I'm working," she said grimly, and pushed back from the table. "I've been assigned to Bobo."

Bo said nothing.

"You've been assigned to a beach stand that Bo is running for me tomorrow," Grace quietly corrected her, then handed her the dishes she was leaving behind. "In the sink, please."

Tosh sighed. "Well, that leaves me with dishpan hands."

Roan turned to him, her eyes bright. "Trade you jobs."

"Nothing doing," said Grace.

Bo slipped past the two of them. "Come on, Mooch," he said. "I'll send him up at bedtime, Grace. Unless David comes," he added with a grin.

"Smelling like a sea rat who's spent time in a garage," said Grace.

"David smells like a sea rat who's spent time in a garage? He must be charming," Tosh remarked.

Roan laughed over her shoulder.

Tosh was the one who was charming, Kate thought.

If only he hadn't come so soon. If only he had let her get her feet on the ground, feel comfortable in her job, and lay to rest the ghost of summers past.

Everyone wandered off then, Marta to bed, Grace and Roan downstairs to the rec room to watch the big-screen TV. While Tosh washed up, Kate read in the breakfast room. Then they moved to the living room. Its furniture was more formal than the big lower-level room, the mantel of its fireplace marble rather than the rec room's rough stone. It had sliding doors that let in a breeze off the ocean. The soft carpet was a good one to stretch out on and read.

Tosh brought a book in from his car. He lay down next to Kate on the floor and turned pages. From time to time he lifted his hand and laid it down on her, smoothing her hair, stroking her wrist.

For months they had read together this way. It

was always soothing, always comforting, and sometimes it had turned quite romantic. But now she wished he'd leave her alone—not for forever, just right now. But she could never explain that to him. She could never explain how she had once imagined she and Justin lying together, reading Beach Patrol stuff.

Tosh had picked up her semaphore manual and was studying the diagrams. Semaphore was the flag signaling system used by the guards. The pictures showed stick figures holding two red-and-white flags in different positions, each position indicating a letter of the alphabet.

Tosh caught Kate watching him. "Can you teach me how?" he said. "I'd love to send you signals."

Kate tried to laugh. She had once dreamed about practicing with Justin: I * M * 4 * U ** R * U * M I N E **

"Of course, I already know a few hand signals," Tosh said, and put down the book. He laid his hand on her thigh and began to massage her gently. Pulling himself up on his side, he let his hand travel farther.

"I—I'm awfully tired," Kate said, but she didn't push him away. He kept touching her softly.

"Is it comfortable on the floor?" Roan asked from the doorway. She showed no signs of embarrassment.

Tosh rolled on his back again. "If you want to

102

try it, there's room on this side," he replied, patting the rug.

Roan laughed, but before she could answer, Grace came in behind her. Grace saw Kate shuffling her papers and Tosh lying flat, with his hands behind his head. "Wouldn't you rather have a bed, Tosh? A bed and even a half-decent pillow?"

Kate was about to protest, not wanting Grace to bear the burden of playing hostess to her friends. But what could she do? Offer to let him sleep with her in her room?

She let Grace lead them upstairs and show Tosh the room next to Kate's.

Roan followed them, then wandered into Grace's room. When she emerged, she said, "Tomorrow I'm using your whirlpool."

"If I let you," said Grace. Then Grace searched the cupboards for some sheets for Tosh. She brought out a nightgown and matching robe for Roan.

The gown was plum-colored silk. Roan's face grew softer at the sight of it. She fingered the gown, then held it, its sheer lace bodice and flow of shimmery material, close to her body.

Kate and Tosh stared at her. Grace said, "You know, you're a beautiful girl."

"How could she not know that?" Tosh asked.

Roan's eyes went from Grace to Tosh, and held there.

"You'd be surprised what people don't know about themselves," Grace said. "Sleep well, Roan. I'm hauling you out of bed at seven a.m."

When Roan had retreated down the steps and Grace had closed her bedroom door, Tosh turned to Kate.

"Maybe you, too, should borrow a nightgown from Grace," he said, his eyes glimmering.

Kate shook her head. "Who wants to toss and turn in lace that itches and silk that makes you sweat? I prefer to be comfortable. And anyway," she added with a mischievous smile, "I sleep in the nude. Good night."

"Good night," he said with a sigh.

EIGHT

Chelsea heard Connor come in the door. She laid her head down quickly on her pillow, though she found it thoroughly, metaphysically gross—being that close to his. She squeezed her eyes shut. I hope they are all dead, she thought.

She listened, trying to keep her breath even, as Connor went in and out of the bathroom, then undressed in the dark. He slipped into bed, trying not to wake her. Chelsea stayed perfectly still, holding her breath as he lowered his head to the pillow.

He didn't notice. Didn't notice! She could smell beer on him; perhaps he had had a little too much and he wouldn't notice till morning. Oh God! She'd have to sleep all night with them right next to her.

He turned his head, nestling in.

"Hhwha?" Connor jerked up, then turned on the lamp. "Agh!"

Chelsea opened her eyes and nearly screamed herself, though she was the one who had laid to rest the twenty-five roaches.

Connor was speechless, pointing at his pillow, his hair flaming up like a small patch of wildfire.

"Hello, dear," Chelsea said cheerily. "Did you forget to do something today?"

"What are they doing here?"

"Dozing?"

"Chelsea!"

"I agree," she said, climbing out of bed to get away from the things. "They're disgusting. I asked you Friday, Saturday, and twice this morning before I left for work, and still you haven't bought a Roach Motel."

"Of course I haven't bought it. Why take out a mortgage on this place, when we can rent it so cheap?" he replied.

"You know what I'm talking about, Connor. I explained it to you three times. Roach Motels are plastic boxes full of chemicals. Roaches climb into them and die."

"Right. I guess I got confused. I kept looking for a roach mausoleum. You know, something with a little monument out front, a quaint marble of one of the little buggers on his back, legs sticking up, and over top, a nice inscription—"

"Stop it! Stop it! Stop it!"

Connor stopped with his mouth wide open.

"It won't work this time, Connor. You can't joke and storytell your way out of it. It's happened once too often."

Grim-faced, Connor picked up his pillow, opened the window, and tossed out the bugs. Then he said, "Would you care to define *it*?"

"I come home tonight, having worked double shift at Face Place, having sketched enough portraits to fill a museum, and I'm hungry, I'm starved, I open the refrigerator, and what's there?"

"Milk?"

"It says milk, but it's empty. It makes me crazy the way you put empty things back on the shelf! All there is in the fridge is an empty milk carton and two roaches who had hopes of being resuscitated in the next century. You promised to go to the store—yesterday. I figured you'd go to the store—today. But why? All year, when it was your turn, you promised to go to the store and usually forgot. What's your excuse this time?"

"Well, it's not an excuse, Chelsea, it's just how it happened. The boys asked me out for pizza, so I stopped worrying about what I was going to eat, so I forgot about going to the store."

"You only think of your own needs, Connor, and I'm sick of it. I cut you a break in New York—"

"Did you?"

"I said to myself, this is a whole new experience for him. The Big Apple. A new job. Lectures at the university."

"Oh, brave new world!" sang out Connor.

"Naturally, I said to myself, he's distracted."

"Being just a poor peasant boy from the old country," Connor observed sarcastically.

"But O.C. is old hat for you," she continued. "And now it's time you take some responsibility. When you do something, you do it really well, Connor. But it's as if you focus on it so much, you forget about time, schedules, everything else that has to be done. And then we end up in a bad way. You're going to have learn to think about what we need as a couple. You're going to have to plan, and follow through."

"Oh, that's great coming from you," said Connor. "You plan all right, you plan big time and leap from one project to the next, never quite finishing anything, leaving all your almost-dones strewn across the landscape. It's colorful, I grant you, but I'm tired of wading in my own living room. I'm surprised you can make out my outline among the clutter."

"It wouldn't be so cluttered if you weren't so pigheaded about taking money from my father. You know he'd pay for us to have a much nicer, bigger place—"

"Well, maybe he should pay for *two* places."

"You know he'd—" Chelsea caught her breath. "What do you mean?"

They looked at each other for a long moment. Then Connor gave a little shrug. Chelsea knew his body language by heart. She knew he was going to try to back away from the statement.

"What I mean is, two places, one to keep everything that, uh, has to be kept, and another, another just for us." He looked up at her hopefully.

"That's not what you meant."

"Then why don't you tell me what I meant," he said tensely.

"You meant we should separate."

"Is that what you think?" he asked.

"I don't know what I think," Chelsea said, dropping her head, staring down at the floor. "I know I need a cool-off time. Maybe I'll just sleep on the porch."

"*I'll* sleep on the porch," he said quickly.

"That eager, are you? You really do want to separate!" she accused him.

He punched the pillow in his hands. "I'm simply being chivalrous. There are mosquitoes out there. And I forgot to buy a mosquito condo!"

"I've had enough!" Chelsea shouted, hot tears rising in her eyes. "I'm going to Grace's." She pulled out a suitcase and started throwing stuff in it. "Grace will have plenty of room for me."

"At first," Connor said quietly.

"Well," said Chelsea, surveying the noontime crowd at Floaters and the constant parade of people on the boardwalk outside, "there must be a lot of girls in O.C. dreaming about having a lifeguard ask them to lunch. None of them, of course, are dreaming about you."

Kate laughed. Floaters was the old hangout for guards at the southern end of the boardwalk. The wooden tables looked as if someone had ice-skated over them. The food was pretty lousy—greasy hamburgers, french fries, and cakes of unknown species of fish being the prime choices.

"Do you like your job?" Kate asked. This was ridiculous. Her best friend had just left her husband, and here she was making small talk. But with all that was going on, they hadn't talked since Friday night, and Kate hardly knew where to begin. "Skip that," she said. "I know you do and I know you're terrific at it. What's going on, Chels? What's going on with Connor?"

"Did we surprise you?"

"No," Kate said honestly.

Chelsea sighed. "It's hard to explain. Connor and I have really different ways of doing things, really different styles, and different beliefs in what is important."

"You've always known that," said Kate.

"I *knew* it," Chelsea said, "but I hadn't experienced it."

"But we all lived in the house together last year. Your rooms were next to each other."

"It's different, Kate," she said. "When you're married to someone and all the spaces in your home are shared spaces, it's different somehow."

She sat back so their waitress could place baskets of food in front of them. The napkins lining their baskets bore an unpromising shimmer of grease.

"Who ordered this?" said Chelsea.

"You did. Go on, about you and Connor."

"It's as if—" Chelsea poked at the fish. "There's enough liquid here to sustain life. You don't think it's still breathing?"

"The tartar sauce usually smothers them," Kate said gently. "Go on."

"When you're married, it's as if you see things under another lens. When you're that close to each other, differences become magnified. What used to be quirky and funny about the other person isn't so quirky and funny anymore."

"But you still love him?"

Chelsea looked away. When she met Kate's eyes again, her own were pink.

"And he still loves you. I know he does!" Kate said quickly.

"Love isn't enough, Kate! We were way too young to get married."

Kate stirred her drink absently. Once upon a time she had believed in happily ever after. But real life and real love were so complicated. "So, what are you two going to do?"

"Have a chill-out time, think about things. I'm not sure what I can change about myself to make it work better. I guess Connor feels the same way." She poked at her fish again. "Do you think Grace minds the extra body on her sofa?"

"If this were last summer, I would've said yes right away. But Grace has changed. Have you noticed?"

Chelsea nodded. "Any day now I expect to see her standing at our end of the boardwalk, raising up her golden lamp like the Statue of Liberty, singing, 'Give me your tired, your poor.' Why do you think she's acting this way?"

"That's what's so strange," said Kate. "I don't think it is an act." She rolled up the remains of her shiny hamburger. "She said something about 'With money comes responsibility,' but I think it's more than that. I think she really needs us around."

"To chase away the ghosts?" Chelsea suggested.

Kate nodded. "I lost Justin. But she lost both

him and her mother. I can hardly imagine how that feels."

They both sat silently for a few minutes.

"Well, I'm sure grateful to her," Chelsea said at last. She began to decorate her uneaten fish with ketchup. "As is that blond girl, I suppose."

"Mmm. Maybe," Kate said. "You must have been really upset last night. Tosh said you didn't recognize him when he answered the door."

"I would have recognized him," Chelsea replied, "but he wasn't supposed to be there, and then when that blond girl in the purple come-on outfit appeared so close behind him, the picture looked wrong, if you know what I mean. I got confused."

"Roan's just a kid," Kate said quickly.

"So you don't think Grace, the new and improved Grace, minds me on her sofa for another night?"

Kate shrugged, then sighed. She had already been thinking about this. There was enough space in her room to put in a cot. But if Chelsea moved in with her, Kate might never find her own bed again.

"Well, there's Tosh's room," Kate said aloud, "and he should be leaving soon."

"In the meantime, you don't want him in with you?"

"I suppose he could sleep on a cot."

"How is it for you?" Chelsea asked. "I've been

so wrapped up in myself, I haven't even asked you. How is it being back here without Justin?"

Kate shook her head, then squished her straw down in her cup. "Chelsea, the thing is I don't feel as if I am without him. I know I have to get past this. I have to accept it. But I still find myself thinking: I have to tell Justin such-and-such. He just doesn't feel dead to me." She blinked back the tears. "Now I know why we have that dreadful practice of open caskets. It's so you can look at the body and say, Yup, he's dead."

Chelsea reached across the table for Kate's hand. "You're still mourning. Is Tosh understanding about that?"

"Oh, he's Mr. Understanding," Kate choked.

"Tonight's memorial service might help you," said Chelsea. "It might make Justin's death more real."

Kate gulped. She hadn't mentioned the service to Tosh, though the announcement had been prominently displayed in this week's *Gazette*. She wondered if Tosh had seen it, and if he were planning to come. The whole beach patrol would be there. She wondered if her new colleagues would be watching her. Was she the only one whose heart just couldn't grasp that he was gone?

"I—I probably shouldn't say this," said Chelsea, "but in a way I envy you. You will always have the dream of you and Justin together. You will always have last summer, the memory of true love, without it being ruined by the usual stupid arguments and thoughtlessness."

"You're right," said Kate, pushing back her chair. "You shouldn't have said that."

NINE

Marta drove her van into the lot at the southern tip of the island, just below the amusement pier. David and Grace said that they would keep an eye out for her, since the service was going to be held on the beach and she would need someone to carry her where her wheels wouldn't. It was quarter to nine and already a large crowd had gathered between the pier and the long stone breakwater that shielded the inlet to the bay. While all the tourists were heading out of the city, marking the end of the Memorial Day holiday with an endless string of headlights, the workers were coming together for their own night of remembering. No breeze stirred the night; still, the air was cold and damp, a fog coming in from the sea. The signal at the end of the breakwater had been activated, sending out a beam of misty light. The long, low sound of the foghorn was, to Marta, the sound of mourning.

She pulled a folded blanket onto her lap, closed up her van, and rolled toward the edge of the paved lot.

"Can't go any farther?" a voice asked from behind her.

Marta recognized the voice immediately and caught herself, just before she started fixing hair that didn't need to be fixed.

She turned. "Oh. It's you."

"Dominic," he said. His hand touched hers, brushed the top of it in a shy kind of greeting.

"Marta," she replied. Her name was about the only thing she could remember at the moment.

"I know."

It annoyed her that this stranger could reduce her to silent idiocy. For better or worse, Marta had always been quick with the tongue, especially when facing off with a guy.

"Did you know Justin?" she asked him.

"No. I just arrived here a few days ago from— from the big city. And I just applied for a job up on the pier."

Marta glanced up at the rides that were glittering softly in the mist.

"I couldn't resist," said Dominic. "The job, I mean. I couldn't resist the job."

Marta stared at him, and he quickly turned his gaze back toward the lights. Could it be,

118

she wondered, that he was feeling as tongue-tied as she?

"They hired me immediately," he said. "You'll never guess what I'm going to be."

"What?"

"Dracula. At Horror Hall."

Marta threw back her head and laughed. How perfect! She could just see him leading tours through the haunted house.

"I think I can pull it off," he said, a bit defensive in the face of her laughter.

"Oh, I think so too," she said quickly.

"What do you mean by that?"

"You'll have girls of all ages screaming for more."

He focused on her as if he were trying to read her face. Was he looking for encouragement? she wondered. But how could he be, if the wheelchair bothered him so?

"Can you take your chair onto the sand?" he asked her.

"No. I'm waiting for friends. One of them will carry me."

"May I?"

"May you?"

"Carry you. I'll be careful."

"I'm warning you," she said. "I had garlic bread for dinner, and I always wear a crucifix around my neck."

He looked, perhaps a little longer and a little lower on her chest than necessary.

"Okay. So I forgot it tonight."

He leaned down, slipping an arm beneath her. "I never bite until the moon is up."

Then he carried her as if she were a china doll. She enjoyed looping her arms around his neck. When he stole a glance down at her at the same time that she gazed up at him, his chin bumped her nose. She laughed, then laughed louder when he stepped in a hole.

Then Marta saw Bo.

Bo waved her over. "David and Grace are looking for you."

"Run and tell them I'm found," she said. "Here is fine, Dominic."

She tossed her blanket on the sand. He attempted to hold her with one hand, which he was strong enough to do, and, with the other, neatly spread the blanket.

"For heaven's sake, drop me," she said.

"I didn't want to get you sandy."

"No problem. It only takes a crane to get me into the bathtub."

He looked at her, frowning.

"That was a joke, Dominic. Not a very good one. Still, it was a joke. Some things are funny about my situation."

He nodded and continued his efforts until he laid her down gently on the perfectly unfolded blanket.

"You know, you're a lucky guy," she said. "If anybody else had treated me as if I were a fragile child, I'd have punched his lights out."

He wiped the fine sheen of sweat from his upper lip. "Would you like me to leave?"

"No, I would like you to sit on this blanket."

Dominic had just settled down next to her when Grace and David arrived. Marta made introductions, wondering if Dominic recognized Grace as the woman behind the binoculars. He didn't give any sign of it. Grace had her hair swept up on her head and looked somewhat older and quite elegant standing next to David.

Marta smiled at both of them, thinking how perfect they were for each other. David had the self-confidence and compassion one saw in a person who had struggled hard in his own life and still came out believing in himself— and others, even those who'd hurt him. His quiet strength and kindness allowed Grace to shine.

Roan and Bo followed Grace and David. Marta smiled to herself. Definitely not the perfect couple. Bo was ignoring Roan, keeping his eyes on the well-brushed Mooch, who was straining at his leash.

When Roan was introduced to Dominic, she looked him over with undisguised interest. It was intriguing to Marta that such an obvious appraisal by a beautiful young girl in no way unnerved him. Only she, Marta, seemed to have that power, and that unnerved her.

"So," Roan said to Dominic, "are you here to cry some crocodile tears?"

David turned his head toward Roan, but said nothing.

"I never met Justin," Dominic replied. "So I'm here just to be with people who miss him."

"I've seen his picture," Roan told him. "Major stud. There will be a lot of women who need comforting tonight."

David leaned around Grace, as if he were going to say something. Grace caught him by the hand and he eased back. He wouldn't get involved unless Grace wanted him to.

Roan continued. "At our house, it's like half mast, if you know what I mean. I don't know how many of them he screwed."

Now Grace turned toward the girl, perhaps a little too quickly. At the same time, a blond-haired boy in a black T-shirt and jeans stepped close to them.

"Roan, why don't you tell Dominic about something you *really* know about," Grace suggested.

"I call them like I see them," said Roan.

"Then you're blind," said Grace, her eyes dark with anger.

"Sorry, Grace," Roan replied. "Tosh filled me

122

in on things. It's a hard night for both you and Kate."

"You make it any harder for Kate," Grace warned, "and I'll have your ass."

"You touch her, I'll have yours and more," said the blond-haired boy.

Grace turned her glare on him.

Dominic was on his feet now.

"Who the hell are you?" Grace asked the boy.

"I'm warning you. You touch her again—"

David stepped in front of Grace. The boy reached in his pocket. Then, before Marta or anyone else could see what the boy had in his hand, the object lay in Dominic's.

The boy looked startled by Dominic's quickness and skill.

Dominic opened the switchblade, examined it, and closed it again.

Marta felt a sick feeling in her stomach. She had seen enough of this stuff as a child in L.A.

Roan said, "She's not the one, Billy. I told you. It was the old lady. The *old lady.* Grace hasn't touched me. She's been . . . almost decent to me."

Billy looked at Roan with his head tilted to one side, as if he were thinking things over. He's faking it, thought Marta. He doesn't know what to do. Then the boy turned to Dominic. He didn't ask for the blade back. He knew better than that.

"I don't need this," said Dominic. He laid it in the boy's hand. "And neither do you."

Billy pocketed the blade and walked away.

When Dominic sat down again, he wouldn't meet Marta's eyes.

"I—I hope that didn't upset you," he said at last.

"Me?" she laughed. "I grew up in L.A., the wrong part of L.A."

He nodded and gazed off at the gathering crowd. Marta wanted to lean against him but didn't.

"Hey, pals and old roomies"—everyone turned around, and Connor looked pleased by the response—"would any of you like to give mild-mannered Clark Kent a few quotes about the dearly departed?" He had his reporter's pad out. "I'm all ears."

"They are big," Bo commented with a smile.

"Connor," said Grace, "this is a memorial service. Try to act appropriately subdued."

"He is, for an Irishman," David said lightly. "The Irish celebrate a person's passing with a wake. Only Christmas is more fun for them."

"Spoken like a good Jewish fellow. But don't you go pretending, David. I've sat shivah. There wasn't any beer, but they found enough other ways to make up for it."

David grinned.

"Now help me out on this. This is my big

124

story, since I've already covered the watermelon-seed spitting contest and the hermit crab beauty pageant. I need some quotes, preferably touching and to the point, from Justin's friends. I can make up any inspiring quotes needed from our dearly departed. After all, I, myself, was nearly deported once."

Everyone laughed.

Connor was relieved. He needed to laugh and be laughed at. Then he saw Chelsea, along with Kate and Tosh, heading toward the group.

"Uh-oh. I'm going to get some powerful quotes now, but I'm not sure they'll be printable."

"Remember why we're here, Connor," Marta advised gently.

He nodded silently and continued to gaze at Chelsea. He wished she didn't look so—so all right. More than all right, she was looking artistic chic. But he should be used to that by now. All the creative energy that was always spurting out in the form of amazing shirts and startling hair thingamabobs had been slowly shaped by the style of New York; she was becoming both original and classy.

Damn. At least her eyes could look puffy. Or she could look like she hadn't slept for three days. Riordan, she's only been gone for one day, he reminded himself. And why, anyway, should he want to live with someone who home-decorated with roaches?

Everyone was looking at Chelsea and seeing how all right she looked. Get ahold of yourself, Riordan—everyone was looking at Kate.

"Hey, Kate. Hey, Kate," people greeted her, some who were from the beach patrol and standing nearby.

"Hi, everyone."

Obviously he couldn't lean on Kate to get him and Chels through this one. She looked pale as a ghost. Maybe it was the lighting. With the weekend tourists gone, the rides on the pier were blinking off one by one. Only the pale purple lights, glimmering along the pier's length, remained lit. They were haloed in the fog, and the rides themselves looked like odd skeletons, animals in fantastic poses. To the right, the signal light at the end of the breakwater made sweeping circles, searching and searching the black sea for something lost.

"Justin Garrett. He was a good man. He was a good friend. He was one of the best damned guards Luis ever had." Everyone smiled a little at this, except Luis, who stood next to the guard who was speaking, his face expressionless. The service had begun.

Speaker after speaker climbed up on the wooden platform and spoke of the Justin each one knew. Justin, the old schoolmate, the big kid defending the little kid on the playground. Justin the practical joker: "He shot at high targets," said the older woman, her voice quivering with laughter and tears. "After all, I was the school principal." Justin the neighbor, helping when no other kids were around to see how much he helped. Justin the savior: the mourners listened as the father of a child that Justin had pulled from the surf struggled to tell his story. He couldn't finish it, and the small boy tried to comfort his father.

"Tears, idle tears," Connor thought as Grace and David cried softly together.

Connor had helped Kate write her term paper on Tennyson. It was as close as he had ever gotten to her, trying to help her through a poem that could have been written just for her. It was a time of closeness for him and Chelsea, too, for they came together trying to comfort Kate. Or maybe they came together haunted by that refrain about "the days that are no more."

He heard the poem in his head, heard Chelsea's voice reading it. "Dear as remembered kisses after death. . . ." Connor glanced over at Kate. Her face looked like a pale moon. The night was cold and her arms were bare and goose-bumped. Tosh was standing directly behind her, but a few inches back, not touching her. It had to be hard for him, Connor reflected, hearing about such a hero and not knowing what to do about the girl this hero had left behind.

Still, Kate needed to be touched right now, Connor was sure of it. Even if Tosh just took her hand, it would help.

Connor slipped his arm around Kate's waist. At the same time, so did Chelsea. They looked at each other across Kate, his arm on top of Chelsea's. Kate leaned back against them, but continued to stare straight ahead, her pale face now coming alive with golden shadows as the bonfire was lit. Connor watched her for a moment, then looked back at Chelsea, who was staring at him. He saw Chelsea's lip tremble. He tightened his fingers around Chelsea's arm.

Maybe if he held on a little longer, he thought, maybe if we both hold on tighter . . . maybe, he thought, but then Chelsea turned to Tosh.

"Kate needs you," she said, and began to withdraw her arm. Connor looked at her uncertainly, then did likewise. Tosh pulled the shivering Kate back to him, wrapping his arms around her as if he were her cape.

The bonfire was raging now, and candles were handed out. One was lit in the big fire and the flame was passed, taper to taper. Connor's lit Kate's. Kate's lit Chelsea's. Chelsea's lit Marta's. Connor saw Bo, sitting by himself, holding on to Mooch. He was about to walk over to him when the blond girl, the tough-looking one, went over. She gently touched Bo on the shoulder and handed him a quivering light.

There was some singing then. The song was only vaguely familiar to Connor. At this point, Justin seemed only vaguely familiar, Connor thought grimly, though he knew that he was very much alive to Kate. Perhaps he was larger than life now. That's how it was when you loved somebody you couldn't live with.

Kate couldn't stop shivering. Tosh had driven her back to the house with the car heat on high. He had rested his hand, palm up, on the seat next to her, so she could take hold of it or ignore it, as she chose.

She didn't know how to begin to choose. How did a person let go and hold on at the same time? She knew that she had to let go of the past in order to take hold of the future, but her hands stayed curled in numb little fists. She felt suspended in an endless and lonely present.

Grace had decided to stay with David that night. When Kate and Tosh arrived home, everyone else was heading down to the rec room to watch an old movie.

"Come on, Kate," Chelsea said. "People are good for you. You need to be with people at times like this."

But being surrounded by people who couldn't really understand how much she had lost made Kate feel all the more isolated. She turned to Tosh. "I need to go upstairs."

He followed her up, uninvited.

When Kate sat down on the bed, Tosh watched her for a moment, then sat down next to her, putting his arms around her. Slowly he began to rock her. Kate leaned against him. He rocked and rocked her, holding her face close to his, letting her tears run over the back of his hand.

When she had stopped crying, he traced her arm with gentle fingers. "Still cold?"

"I can't seem to get warm. Though you are helping a lot," she said. "Thanks."

"I know something else that might warm you," he told her. He pulled the light quilt off the bed, wrapping it around her, then went over to the pile of things stashed beneath his cot. From a box he pulled out two brandy snifters and a small metal frame with a candle set in it.

After clearing a space on her bedside table, Tosh set up the brandy warmer. From his suitcase he took a bottle of brandy and, opening it, poured the gold liquid into each of the bulb-shaped glasses. He lit the candle and turned off Kate's bedroom lamp.

It had soothed her, somehow, watching this little ceremony. Kate found herself staring into the yellow flame as she had the bonfire. But this time, the face of Justin seemed to be on the other side of the flickering warmth, and she couldn't quite reach through to him.

Tosh set a glass in the holder above the candle, allowing it to heat. Kate watched as a pale steam rose from the brandy and a delicious smell warmed the air.

Tosh took the warmed glass and set it in her hands, cupping his beneath hers, as if the two of them were holding a flower. Kate bowed her head over the glass and breathed in deeply. The vapor both burned and soothed.

She looked up at Tosh. "Try it," he said softly.

Kate sipped the golden liquid. She closed her eyes and sipped some more.

Then Tosh set the other glass over the flame. Kate watched as the fog swirled out of the glass. The whole room became fragrant.

Tosh piled pillows behind them so they could lean against the bed's headboard. For a long time they sipped and didn't speak. Kate had nothing to say, and perhaps he knew that words wouldn't touch her now. What she needed now was warmth.

Kate gazed up at Tosh, watching the flicker of candle flame on his face. Then she reached up and touched his cheek ever so lightly. His face bent down toward hers; their lips brushed. His kiss was unbearably tender, and the tips of his fingers, framing her face, were warmer than the brandy. She craved his warmth, and when she

131

opened her lips, he gave her more.

His hands moved softly down her neck, down to the buttons on her blouse. Kate shivered. Nothing could be warmer than skin against skin, she thought.

She sighed when she felt his bare chest against hers. He burned through all the cold, and his kisses became more insistent. She felt him reach for the zipper on her jeans and ease it down. The flame that had been working slowly through her was hot now. She wrapped her legs around him. She twisted in his arms. Suddenly she was fire in his arms.

"Kate," he said.

And then she wasn't sure whose voice that was, what fire it was, what face she was seeing in the flames.

She went limp in his hands.

Tosh stared at her, his dark blue eyes burning into her with all the heat she had felt. But she could only blink up at him now.

He bowed his head and rolled off her.

"Tosh," she said quietly.

"What?" The word came out bitter and tight. She could hardly blame him.

There was a long silence.

"I—I know I'm making it so very hard for you. I know I have to make up my mind. But to do that, I have to be thinking clearly. If we make love, it should be a choice made by both heart and head."

He didn't say anything.

"I can't make that kind of choice now. Soon. Soon, I will, I promise."

He nodded grimly and pulled the quilt up around her. She caught his hand and kissed it. He kissed hers. Whispery soft kisses.

But all she could think of was the first time Justin had pulled her hand up to his mouth.

TEN

Eleven thirty Thursday morning Chelsea made up her mind. She needed her sketch pads. All of them. She had been staring out the window of her room. It was a room with a view, a very good view of the apartment she and Connor were supposed to be sharing.

She had watched Connor go to work that morning, and Tuesday and Wednesday as well. In this early part of the summer, when O.C. was empty midweek, most workers had a light schedule. But the *Gazette* was still published every Friday, just in time for the weekenders, so Connor was kept busy. At least, he looked busy.

Chelsea wondered what kinds of stories he had been assigned. It seemed strange not to know what he was working on, what he was thinking about. He wasn't thinking about her—

135

she had noticed that he never glanced up at Grace's house.

She needed her sketch pads. It would be best to get them while Connor was out.

She pulled close the curtain, then stopped, staring at her left hand as if it wasn't hers. She turned slowly her wide, gold ring, then slipped it over her knuckle and gazed down at her bare hand.

What if they hadn't gotten married? Chelsea wondered. What if she were still a single woman?

How romantic it would have been, returning to Ocean City, finding him here again. All winter he would have been hoping and waiting for her. How they would have rushed together! There would still have been that hint of danger, the fear that at any time he might be caught by Immigration, making each moment they spent together precious.

When each moment is precious, she thought, remembering to buy toilet paper and put out the trash becomes rather unimportant. And when you choose, as she had, not to make love until you're married, each brush of the hand, each stolen glance and shy kiss becomes unbearably sweet and full of promise.

But, really, how long can something like that last? More important, how had the romance died so quickly? She and Connor had married too young, that was the most obvious answer.

She needed her sketch pads. Drawing was

how she dealt with life—and Grace had been wondering where all her paper bags were disappearing to.

There were clothes and other things Chelsea needed to get as well. She should fetch them as quickly as possible. Tosh was around that morning, but she was reluctant to ask his help. She couldn't explain why. He was such a nice guy and so perfect for Kate; probably he was more right for Kate than Connor was for herself. Still, Chelsea couldn't warm up to him.

Glancing at her watch, Chelsea turned away from the window and ran downstairs. In the kitchen she snatched large plastic bags, then hurried across the lot to her old apartment.

It was a shock at first, seeing the place just as she had left it. She'd assumed that Connor had immediately put the place in order. But her magazines were still mixed in with his, her dirty shirts still had their arms wrapped around his, their mugs sat together on the kitchen counter—next to a Roach Motel.

For a moment Chelsea's resolve wavered. Then she whirled through the apartment, snatching up sketch pads, charcoals, pastels, underwear, a pink boa, shoes, two jewelry boxes, Grape-Nuts, a silver pinwheel, glitter tubes, pretzels, bubble bath, tapes, and, of course, Huge-and-Hairy, the plant.

She piled them by the front door, then

searched the room again, spotting the photo album beneath a drift of newspapers. Inside the album were pictures that belonged to both of them. Chelsea traced the gold heart embossed on the leather cover, wondering if it was fair to take something that belonged to Connor, too.

I bought the album, I'm taking it, she said to herself.

When she picked it up, a flurry of photographs fell out. Then she remembered: while she had bought the album, she never quite got around to putting the photos in it.

Chelsea knelt down to pick up the photos. There were snapshots from last summer: Connor in his doughnut days, Connor in his hard-hat days, Connor on the beach—laughing at her, flirting with her as she took the picture. Chelsea swallowed hard.

Here was Connor in a suit. Their wedding. Kate had taken these pictures with Chelsea's camera. And she had caught Chelsea and Connor in the church when they thought they were alone. They had thought that everyone else had gone on to the reception and, seizing the moment, were making out big time by the Blessed Mother statue. It was a funny picture, Mother Mary watching with blessed approval while Connor groped the huge white dress.

Now tears rolled down Chelsea's face. She wiped them away quickly, stuffed the photos back in the album—all but the one of Connor on the beach—then put the album back with the newspapers.

She was just tucking Connor's picture in her pocket when she heard a key in the door lock. Quickly she ran her hands over her cheeks.

Connor came in expecting a floor, not a pile, in front of him. He stepped on the pretzels, then crunched the pinwheel. He tried to keep from tumbling into Huge-and-Hairy and ended up with the boa looped around one leg.

Chelsea stared at him. "You're home," she said.

"So are you," said Connor. There was a hopeful light in his eyes.

"Just briefly," she told him, then regretted how lightly and quickly she had delivered the punch.

Connor stared down at her pile. He didn't say anything for a few moments. Was he going to beg her to stay?

"You're taking my green socks," he said.

"Connor, you haven't worn those socks since the day I bought them. You said they glowed in the dark and attracted light moths. And you know they match my shorts." She pointed to a pair in the pile.

"You're taking everything," he said.

"I'm taking what I need."

"You're taking everything you need," he replied. "So this is it, the end for us?"

"Don't get melodramatic."

"I was asking a simple question," he said. He hadn't moved from the spot where he had first entered the apartment.

"You were the one who suggested the separation," she reminded him. "And you were right. You and I both need time to sort things out, to figure out what we can change and what we can't."

"How much time?" he asked.

"How much?" She looked at him blankly—she honestly had no idea.

"I just want to know so I can mark it on my calendar," he said. "You know how I forget things. Well, I'm starting to write them down now." He stepped around the pile, still dragging the boa with him, and picked up a calendar. "See here, there's 'Rent due today. Pick up milk. Buy a new Roach Motel'—that's checked off. So, where do I write in 'Chelsea comes back'?"

Chelsea stared over his shoulder at June, with its big picture of fish—fish dangling from hooks.

"I mean, I was just wondering when," he said with a small quiver in his voice. He kept his back to her, waiting for an answer.

"I can't tell you, Connor," she said softly. "I don't know when."

"Okay." He took a deep breath. "Okay." He turned to face her again. "Then maybe you can tell me what the rules are."

"The rules?"

"Am I allowed to call you?"

"That's totally up to you," she said. "Only—"

"Only?"

"I need a little time to myself right now."

"How long is a little time?" he asked; then he read her face. "Never mind," he muttered. "Let's keep to the rules. Am I allowed to see other people?"

"Of course you can see other people. We both need friends."

His eyes narrowed. "To be more specific, can I see other women?"

The question caught Chelsea by surprise. She didn't know why she hadn't thought about it before. It was just that she had no desire to be with any other man and she had somehow assumed that he . . . well, she had assumed wrong.

"There are no rules, Connor!" she said angrily. "You are free to do whatever you want, absolutely free! We both are."

Then she threw her stuff into the plastic bags and wondered why, being free as she was, it felt as if the walls were falling in on her.

Grace reached for her bedside clock to see how long she had lain there. She had been musing over all the changes that had occurred in her life and the new title David had given her: Grace Caywood, Proprietress. Proprietress and Mother

Hen, he had said, laughing. Hardly, she thought. Couldn't be, she thought. Whatever happened to Racey Gracie?

But here she was, running some kind of half-way house. Who would have believed it? Grace playing mother to little brother. Grace offering a sisterly hand to Marta and a shoulder to the mourning Kate. Grace taking in one unrequited lover, Tosh; one runaway, Roan; and one un-happy bride, Chelsea. Not to mention the fact that she was attempting to reform Mooch.

Mooch. That's why she couldn't sleep. She shouldn't have blasted him earlier in the evening. Poor, salt-soaked creature with seaweed caught in his tail, he didn't know why she had yelled. All he had done was swim in the bay. He smelled as if he had swum too close to the fishing boats.

Three twenty A.M., the glowing clock said. Grace sighed and pulled herself out of bed. She couldn't rest till she knew that Mooch was safe with Bo.

She tiptoed downstairs, checking the living room and kitchen first, then moving silently to-ward Bo's door. It was closed. She tapped lightly. If Bo were awake, she'd give him time to answer her knock, out of respect for his privacy. But there was no response, so she cracked open the door. "Mooch? Mooch?"

All she heard was Bo's soft breathing.

She slipped down to the next level, hoping to find Mooch sacked out on the lumpy sofa in the rec room. He wasn't. Now she was really getting worried. There weren't many other places to look. Unless Marta had become a recent convert, Grace knew the dog wouldn't be with her. Then she saw that Roan's door was open about a foot. She stood outside and called softly again. "Mooch?"

She heard a whimper. It was Mooch's apologetic, baby whimper. Grace opened the door wider and the smell hit her full force. There he was, stretched out most luxuriously on Roan's bed.

Roan was gone.

Grace turned on the light and glanced around the room in disbelief. Some of the clothes Grace had bought Roan were scattered about. Perhaps she was planning to sneak back in.

"Where'd she go?" Grace hissed.

Mooch, who had been hoping for kiss, slurp, and make up, now stuck his head under the pillow.

Grace hurried upstairs and pulled on jeans and a sweater. She was torn between anger at Roan for sneaking out and fear that she was in serious trouble. There was a lot Grace didn't know about Roan, but one thing she was sure of: she was a girl who could get herself in deep. Scooping up her car keys, Grace rushed out of the house. First stop, Tenth Street.

She drove through three red lights. If a cop caught her, fine, he could help her find Roan. Just as she turned onto Tenth Street, Grace cut her lights and engine, and nosed up into a parking space. If Roan saw or heard her coming, she might bolt.

Grace slipped a can of Mace into her pocket. Marta seemed to think that Billy the Switchblade Kid wasn't all that tough. Even so, a couple drinks or "a little drugs"—whatever that stupid phrase meant—could transform a first grader into an adult-sized threat.

Grace moved quietly along the street and up the ramp to the boardwalk. The town itself was silent, its neon names and shapes extinguished. A moon rose high above it, washing the wooden buildings in white light. Grace was the only ghost walking the boardwalk.

Under the boardwalk, she thought.

Of course, if Roan wasn't there, she had the whole town to search. Just what she was in the mood for tonight. But Grace felt confident; she knew about under the boardwalk near the bathhouses on Tenth Street. In fact, she knew the best spot between the boardwalk supports.

She walked to that spot ever so softly, then leaped down to the sand.

Roan was startled. Her large brown eyes were that of an animal trapped in its den.

"Well, well, well," said Grace.

The guys Roan was with, including the one who was grabbing at her chest, quickly recovered from the surprise. Two moved out from under the boards and stood threateningly close to Grace. They were several years older than Billy the Kid, who had stayed beneath the boards with Roan. In fact, Grace thought they were older than herself; certainly, they were bigger. Clearly, they were trouble.

"This is cozy. Three guys and you, and a lot of beer. A *lot* of beer," Grace observed. "Hope you've got a lot of condoms, too. Hope you're not a fool," she said. "Sorry that you have to share her, Billy."

At that, Billy came out, his eyes blazing.

"Leave the blade in the pocket," Grace told him calmly, though her heart was beating fast. Obviously she was outnumbered. But all three guys were slowed by the alcohol, and she thought she knew how to play them. How to play Roan, that was another question. How to get her out from under the boardwalk and safely home, Grace hadn't the foggiest notion.

Did Roan realize what three semidrunk guys could do to her? Did she know enough not to trust older guys who had nothing better to do than play with a young down-and-out girl? Maybe she did and she just didn't care. Maybe she thought it was exciting. "Do you think you deserve these guys?" Grace asked

Roan. "Or is this some kind of fun for you?"

When Roan didn't answer, Grace said, "That's a real question, Roan. I'm not here to set you straight, then drag you home. That's what I came to do, you must have guessed that. But I'm smart enough to see I'm outnumbered. I'll leave without you, but I'd like to leave with an answer. Why are you doing this?"

"You don't know what I've been through!" Roan replied angrily.

"You're right. Why don't you tell me?"

Roan rose up on her knees and Grace thought she was going to reply, but then the girl's eyes flicked over to one of the guys. He began circling Grace, looking her up and down. His breath was stale with the smell of beer.

"I owe you nothing," Roan said.

"Right again. You earned your keep working at the beach stand."

"So why don't you leave me alone?" Roan cried.

The guy stopped circling. "Maybe she wants what you want, Roan. All women want it," he said, rubbing up against Grace.

Grace stepped aside coolly and kept her eyes on Roan. "Why? Because, sweetie, I'm earning a Girl Scout merit badge."

Roan didn't blink.

"Because I want to make the world a better place?"

"Bull."

"Okay. Because I screwed up once," Grace said, her voice husky. "I let someone down. Someone who needed me."

"Guilt," Roan said with satisfaction.

"In a nutshell. Now I've answered your question, how about you answering mine—honestly," she added.

Roan slowly blinked and set her mouth in a straight line.

Grace knew it was a lost cause.

"Okay, I'm going. I just want to tell you one thing. Drunks don't know how to say no," Grace said. "And drunks don't know how to protect themselves when they say yes."

Roan frowned a little.

"Look out for yourself, Roan. Look out for yourself, because I can't"—Grace's voice shook a little—"and these guys won't." She started off. Behind her she heard the soft chuckling of Roan's companions. Grace suddenly realized how weary she was. Heart weary. It seemed a major effort to walk to the boardwalk steps and cross over to the street.

Grace didn't turn around when she heard the scrape of sandy footsteps on the sidewalk behind her. She was too tired to respond with fear. She didn't turn around when the long shadow caught hers. At the last minute she tightened her grip on her can of Mace.

"You're walking too fast," Roan complained.

Grace swung around and the girl swayed a little on her feet.

"You're drunk."

"Probably," said Roan. "Why else would I follow you?"

"Why else?" Grace echoed.

"I'm beat," Roan replied, and suddenly sounded very young. "Really tired. Could I sleep, uh, anywhere, maybe outside on your terrace?"

Grace sighed. "You can sleep in your room," she replied, unlocking the car door for her, "if you can stand the smell of wet dog and fish."

When they had driven two blocks, Roan said, "Do you really want to know how it's been for me?"

Grace wasn't sure she did anymore; she feared she was in over her head. "Yes, I want to know," she lied.

"I was living with my mom. My dad walked out on us, years ago. I hardly remember him—and I don't care that he left, I don't. Mom stayed. But she's got—you know—problems."

"Does she drink?" Grace guessed.

"A little, but that's not it really. It's the boyfriends."

"What about the boyfriends?"

"One after another," said Roan.

"That can be hard—on both of you."

"I don't mind the one after another. The

148

thing is, Mom's not enough for them."

"Not enough?" Grace's grip tightened on the wheel. "What are you saying?"

"I'm saying Mom's not enough for some of them. And when she's asleep . . ."

"Yes?" said Grace.

Roan closed her eyes.

Grace ran a red light and didn't notice it till she was well past. She drove Roan home in silence.

Roan let out her breath. At last she was alone. Her bed was freshly made over and two aspirin lay on the table next to it. Grace had closed the curtains, telling Roan she could sleep in.

Roan shimmied out of her damp clothes and into Grace's short, silky gown. She wished she could slip into sleep just as easily. She had that strange kind of dizzy, floating feeling that made her long for sleep but wouldn't let her.

Grace's question hovered in the air. It was like a streamer off the back of an airplane, the kind that flew over the beach. Only it was flying around and around her head, trailing behind it: "Do you think you deserve this?"

What *did* she deserve? More than she had gotten in life, a hell of a lot more! Look at Grace. How easy she had it! And how free she was! Look at Kate and all she had. A glamorous life-guard job, a convertible, a dead hero, and lots of sympathy—not to mention Tosh chasing her around, patiently waiting for his chance. Life wasn't fair.

I deserve more, Roan thought, more than three creeps under the boardwalk and wondering where the next meal is coming from.

She folded her arms across her stomach and hunched over. She was hungry and tired. She began to rock herself, but that made her dizzy. She needed food to soak up the alcohol in her.

Switching off her light, she crept out of the room and felt her way to the stairs. When she got to the middle level, it was easier to see. She headed toward the kitchen and realized the light was on in the breakfast room beyond it. Was Kate up, she wondered, getting ready for her run and swim before work? What would Miss All-American Goody-Good think when she smelled the beer on Roan?

I'll just snatch a loaf of bread and leave, Roan thought. She tiptoed in, crouched down, and slid open the bread drawer.

"Couldn't sleep?"

Roan looked over shoulder. Tosh. In shorts only, wrinkled shorts he had probably slept in. She eyed him up and down, and he studied her as well. She liked the way he looked at her, taking in details. Standing up slowly, she turned toward him and began to untwist the wire around the bread bag. "Sleep? I guess not," she said.

"Is everything all right?"

She gave a little shrug. She knew how to keep silent, how to make a guy wonder till he asked some more.

"Do you want to talk?" Tosh asked, moving toward her. "I'm a good listener."

"I don't know," she said. "I don't know if I'm ready."

He cocked his head. "Give it a try," he urged, then moved closer.

"It's Grace."

"What about Grace?"

"She's making my life miserable."

He was standing next to her now at the counter, his hand resting lightly on hers. "How so?"

"She's so strict! She's like my stepmother, and I had all I could take from that woman. I can't put enough miles between my stepmother and me."

"You used to live with your stepmother?"

"She hates me!" Roan exploded. "She hates me because my father still loves me, loves me more than the children he had by her. Don't you see? I had to leave."

"You've had a rough time," Tosh said, rubbing her wrist with one finger.

"Why does Grace make it even rougher for me? I'm old enough to take care of myself. I don't need her to lecture me on condoms and alcohol."

Tosh smiled a little. "I would like to have heard that lecture." Then his face grew more serious. He looked into Roan's eyes. "I think, perhaps, Grace is remembering her own experiences. She's had a tough time. She's a recovered alcoholic, you know."

"Grace is? Really?" Roan ran her tongue over her lips. "Well, she has a dark secret after all. I wondered why this house was so dry."

"But you're not . . . not exactly dry tonight."

"No, I'm not," Roan said lightly. "I've been a bad girl."

"Have you?"

"And now I'm hungry."

"Are you?" Tosh's eyes were a brilliant blue.

"Very hungry."

She felt his fingers curling around her wrists.

"Do you trust me?" he asked softly.

She tilted her mouth up to him, and his came down swiftly to meet it.

His mouth was hot and hard. In her head, Roan heard a high, whining sound. Damn the beer! Then she realized it wasn't her brain going off, but an alarm clock, Kate's alarm clock in the room above them. She and Tosh pulled away from each other at the same time.

Then she laughed. Picking up the bread, she slung it over her shoulder like a little sack. "See you around," she said, and she scurried out of the kitchen, down to her room below.

ELEVEN

With arms working and back flexing, Marta sped down the boardwalk, exulting in the speed gathered by sheer muscle power. "Officer, arrest that woman for speeding!" Connor shouted as she zipped past him, laughing.

"Can't catch her," the policeman answered.

No one could catch her this evening. Except Dominic.

How surprised she had been when he called the clinic at noon. She told him she was working days this weekend. He was working nights. But there was one hour, five to six, his dinner break, when yes, she was free to meet Count Dracula.

"Look at you," the Count said softly when she pulled up in front of Horror Hall. "You're damp and kind of shiny."

She had been given more complimentary descriptions, but this would have to do.

"Look at *you*," she replied, laughing. "You're either ready to bite a neck or sing opera."

Actually, he looked quite handsome in his white ruffled shirt and sweeping black cape. His dark hair was slicked back. Shadows had been colored in around his eyes, making them all the more mysterious.

"I've taken out my teeth," he said.

"Then how are you going to eat dinner?" she asked.

He smiled at her, a smile that could have won its way into the bedrooms of many victims, she thought. Then he turned his back to her. When he whirled around again, his fangs were in place.

"Eee!" she said. "*Show-off!* Let's compare notes. I drew one pint for the bank, plus twenty-five cc's for testing today. How much blood did you get?"

"I wasn't hungry," he said, "till now."

She raised an eyebrow at him.

He grinned, then slipped the fangs out of his mouth, pocketing it.

"Doesn't your chair have a motor?" he asked, resting his hand on the back of it.

"I don't use one. I prefer to wheel myself."

He nodded, then coming around behind her, tried to push the chair.

"I wheel myself," she told him.

"I know you usually do, but since I invited you out tonight—"

Her chair tilted forward. He was pushing, she was holding the wheels still. He persisted, she held on.

Both faces grew stormy.

"I said I wheel myself," she replied, teeth clenched.

He let go. "Sorry."

The growing confidence, the little bit of playfulness he had shown, was gone now. She regretted that, but he had to learn.

"So, where to?" she said.

"Wherever you like," he replied.

"Well, where would you like to go?" she asked him.

"What's your favorite place?" he asked back.

"Oh, good Lord!" Marta cried. "Pick a place, any place."

"I like Tex-Mex."

"I like Chinese."

"Do you want to get a pizza?"

"Great!"

They moved through the crowd on the pier, side by side. The first time the space narrowed, he let her take the lead; the second time, he took it. Marta was aware of him keeping track, trying hard to keep their score even. It got tricky as they merged onto the boardwalk. When it happened to be much more convenient for her to pass through, but it was his turn, he went anyway. They collided. He swore softly and went hopping around on one foot.

Marta laughed, though there was a small lump in her throat.

"Sorry," she said. "It's really not so difficult. Just imagine that you're walking with a very fat woman."

"I wish I could walk and see your face at the same time," he said.

Marta swallowed.

"I shouldn't have said that." He looked away, staring up at the old pier ballroom as if he had never noticed it before.

Marta reached up, pulling his face down to hers. "I wish I could see your face too," she said.

His eyes met hers and she smiled into them.

"Since you're being such a gent, would you treat me?" She pointed toward the domed building just off the boardwalk. It housed kiddy rides. "Would you buy me a ticket for the carousel?"

"The carousel? Sure."

Riding the carousel was Marta's favorite thing to do in all of Ocean City. It was the first thing she had done when her father brought her here seven years ago. Her father, who would never win awards for sensitivity and imagination, had guessed at what his crippled daughter needed—motion. To love motion so that she'd want motion again.

The first spring day the carousel opened, he had brought her here and set her on a horse.

156

She remembered clinging to the brass pole, frightened out of her wits, having to rely on her arms, not her legs, to keep her saddled. Luis stood by, but he wouldn't touch her. After numerous rides on the merry-go-round, which she came to love, there were excursions to the little whip. Then bumper cars. Then the roller coaster. That summer they worked their way through Ocean City's amusement parks. Her father had thrown up several times (made her swear not to tell anyone), and Marta's arms grew stronger and stronger.

But this is where she always came back to. She rode a pony before setting off to college last year. She'd do the same before setting off to med school. This was the place of beginnings for her.

"Marta? Marta, which animal? Do you have a favorite?"

Dominic was pointing like a kid at the zoo as the animals whirled by—a rooster, a pig, a giraffe.

"It has to be a pony. They're the only ones that go up and down," she said. "See, on the two inside rings."

He nodded. Then, when the ride stopped, he swept her up in his arms and dashed on, a little boy determined to get first choice of the horses. A child cried, "Daddy, there goes Dracula. Dracula's riding with us!"

"Dracula, you look quite dashing on your steed," Marta said when he was seated on the pony next to hers. She felt the familiar tingle when the warning bells sounded, and the little tingle of the breeze as the carousel started. She watched Dominic's face, and he watched hers, illuminated against the turning background of darker faces and slices of light.

The ride is always over too soon, thought Marta.

She slid off into his arms. Then they hurried up the boardwalk to Pizzaz.

"I wish I could take you on the carousel three more times and on every other ride tonight," Dominic said as he slid into the wooden seat across from her. He laid the pizza on the table between them, then brought back two sweating glasses. "I'm sorry I have to work."

"It's just as well," Marta replied. "The clinic can be a madhouse Friday and Saturday evening—as you well know. I told them to call if they needed me."

"You're dedicated."

She smiled. "It's easy to be dedicated when you love your work."

"Dr. Salgado," he said, enjoying the sound of it. "Dr. Salgado, you're wanted in O.R."

"First I have to make it into med school," Marta told him. "Which won't be easy," she added. "There's this thing called organic chemistry standing between me and those corpses. How about you, Dominic?"

"I'm a fresh-blood guy myself," he said, flicking back his cape.

She laughed. "I mean, what do you want to do? What are your dreams?"

"I just finished high school, Marta, though I'm older than you."

She nodded.

"I was a dropout. Then I decided to drop back in." He shrugged. "I guess I'm just learning to dream. It's . . . scary . . . allowing yourself to hope again. You can get carried away."

"So get carried away," she said.

"First, I have a debt to pay."

There was that look again, the shadow that came over him.

Marta chewed thoughtfully. Should she ask him more questions? Perhaps she'd only be dredging up old pain. Still, she got the feeling that there were things he wanted to tell her, and she was somehow supposed to figure out how to give him the chance.

"Is it much money that you owe?"

"Money?" He shook his head sadly. "If it was just money . . ."

She waited for him to go on, but he didn't.

"Dominic, where are you from? A big city, you said before. But you don't talk like an East Coaster."

"L.A."

"L.A.? That's where I'm from. Well, I told you

159

that the other night." Marta sat back in her chair. So. Maybe this was part of the strong pull she felt. A shared home, if such a place could be considered home.

"What school did you go to?"

"E. Lee, then Lincoln."

Marta sat up straight. "I went to Edgar Lee! Small world . . ." she said with wonder. Then her eyes narrowed.

"You knew that! That's why you stared at me so when I first saw you on the boardwalk. And then at the clinic—"

"I didn't know you, Marta."

"How many nineteen-year-old Hispanic girls from L.A. in wheelchairs are there? You must have made the connection."

"I didn't know you, Marta."

"And I didn't know you," she said. "But you must have remembered the incident. The gang shooting on the school steps? Lousy shots, those Snake Heads. You remember their symbol—a snake head with a grinning skull between the fangs. They killed Christina. I was luckier. How could you not remember that?"

"I'm older than you."

Marta frowned. "Still . . ."

"And I didn't hang around school much."

"But you remember the Snake Heads?"

"Yes."

"Oh." She got a wry smile on her face. "I see

how it is now. Of course. Rather self-centered of me, I must say."

He looked up at her. "What?"

She took his hand. "Try to understand. I thought people would always remember me, and my story. When something happens like that to you, when your whole life is shaken up—shot up—you think that other people are affected too. Your world is turned upside down, and you assume that theirs is, well, at least tilted.

"But it was really only my tragedy," she continued, "and there are tragedies every day in L.A. My father took me away from there as soon as I was out of the hospital. Why should anyone remember?"

Dominic's eyes were liquid with tears.

"Don't," she said. "Don't, Dominic. It's long past time for that."

His head bowed. He was still holding her hand.

She gripped his hand tighter. "You know, we have something in common," she said. "Not only are we big-city kids, we're survivors. We're strong."

He still wouldn't look up.

"And if you don't cut it out," she added, "I'll prove it by making you arm-wrestle me. Right here. I would certainly hate to humiliate you."

He let go of her hand then, and they ate in silence.

She wondered what he was thinking. Was he recalling some tragedy in his own life? Did she remind him of someone he once knew—perhaps someone he had loved—but left just when she needed him? Maybe that was the debt he owed.

"Dominic, I'm sorry."

He looked up at her, startled.

"I'm sorry for whatever memory I've stirred up. I wouldn't knowingly cause you pain."

He swallowed hard.

"You okay?" she said, passing her hand lightly over his.

He nodded.

"May I escort you back to Horror Hall?"

They said little along the way. No doubt he was now glad he could walk without looking at her face. He probably wouldn't ask her out again. After all, most guys didn't look forward to dates in which they were reduced to tears.

"I'd love to stop in and see your latest torture device," she said cheerfully, "but I had better roll on."

"I'm sorry I have to work," Dominic said.

"No problem."

"I'll call you," he said.

Sure, she thought as she wheeled away.

Just as well. There was some dark and terrible pain in Dominic, and she doubted that she could heal it. Get away while you can, girl, she thought. Still, she stopped to look back one more time at the cardboard house with its rubber bats, its nylon cobwebs, and— he had turned to watch her leave—one truly haunted guy.

TWELVE

"Help, help, I'm drowning! Hey, babe! Lifeguard lady! Come wrap your saving arms around me."

Where was Jaws when you needed him? Ignoring the two guys who found themselves so very entertaining, Kate scanned the water, ten seconds to the left, ten seconds to the right. Her hair hung in a braid down her back, still salty and damp from her early-morning swim. Wisps of it were picked up by the light breeze. She loved the softness of the air. It was a glittering blue, easy-rolling day.

The first day Kate had climbed up onto her own lifeguard chair, she felt like a child playing king of the hill, standing tall, surveying her territory. *From my sandy feet to the blue horizon, I solemnly swear to guard the lives of my people,* she had said to herself. Justin would have laughed.

This Saturday in June the ocean was still a chilly temperature, and most of the bathers were in no deeper than their knees. A few kids, whose fingers must have been Popsicles by now, were waist deep and playing Marco Polo. Some older guys were staging chicken fights, and a middle-aged couple played water Frisbee.

Only one man was a good distance out, and Kate kept a sharp eye on him. He was one of those raft people, content to drift to England if she'd let him. Every ten minutes or so, she had to stand up and whistle at him. He'd lift his head, see that she meant him, give a friendly wave, and paddle into the shallower water. Then the whole routine would start over again.

Luis had stopped by on his way to the next stand, where he was covering for a lunch break. "Raft people," he grumbled. "This kind of sea brings them out. You know, you won't always have it so easy," he reminded Kate.

"You keep promising me," she said.

Ten seconds to the left, ten to the right. Even on an easy day, it was important to maintain the pattern. Last night Tosh had said she was doing it in the mall. "Which one of these shoppers are you going to rescue?" he had teased.

She had worked nine days straight and figured she was probably scanning in her sleep as well. But the long week had earned her a Sunday off, and that was something to be savored. Sunday in the sun with Tosh.

Damn, there he goes again! Kate was getting a little weary of this game with raft man. Apparently his wife was too. At least, Kate assumed she was his wife. The thin, older woman stood knee-deep in ocean foam and had been watching the man like a hawk. Kate guessed that the woman couldn't swim. She recognized the rigid look of someone who wouldn't let a wave push her in or out, a woman afraid to give up any ground to an ocean with which she couldn't negotiate.

Feeling frustrated, Kate bobbed up and gave a shrill blast of her whistle. The Frisbee couple, the four guys having chicken fights, the two drowning bimbo boys, Marco and all the shivering Polos looked up quickly. The man on the raft did not.

Kate gave another hard blast. He continued to ignore her. Anger bubbled up inside her. She tossed aside her sunglasses. She was going to have to pull this guy in.

Blowing three sharp whistles to signal the guards on either side of her, Kate leaped to the sand, yanked up her buoy, and sprinted to the water. She was about to dive into the first shallow wave when the old woman cried out, "Help him, help him! Save him, please!"

Kate spun around. The old woman, unable to

swim, was pushing deeper into the waves. The water battered her back, swirling around her frail body. Kate hesitated, about to reassure her: this was going to be a lecture, not a rescue. Then the old woman cried, "His heart. I know it's his heart."

Kate plunged into the waves and swam with all she had. Her strokes were strong and sure, but each meter seemed like a mile. As she swam, she kept her bearings, slipping under a wave, then targeting the raft again. Twenty-five more meters, twenty, fifteen—

And then he went under, sliding off the raft into water over his head.

Swiftly Kate closed the gap between her and the raft. Sucking down air, she dove. But he wasn't where she thought he would be. Kate thrashed around in the dark. She couldn't find him. She couldn't find him!

Please . . . let me find him.

Can't find him.

Keep your head, Kate.

Can't find him. Can't.

Her eyes burned in the brown salt sea.

Can't find him, help me find him—there!

Her arm slipped under the man's chin and she dragged him up, her lungs ready to burst, a metallic taste in her mouth. The man was breathing—hoarse, convulsed breath. His skin was cold and shone with a strange pallor. She felt as if she were holding a fish.

She couldn't do CPR here. She had to get him in.

Kate swam, one arm around the man, her lungs still burning and sucking up air whenever they could.

Then she saw the man's wife. My God, what was that woman doing, bobbing through the waves? She'd be under next. Where would Kate find the strength for two? She needed help. She needed Justin. Justin. Justin!

He was there. He had the man and Kate. Luis was there.

"Wife!" Kate said, then swam for her.

The woman was hysterical, and Kate had to fight to control her, then had to fight to keep her head up. She got her in to shore and held her tightly while Luis and the other guard gave CPR.

It took forever or it took seconds, Kate didn't know. The wail of the Jeep's siren sent sea gulls screeching upward. Paramedics leaped out and went to work.

But suddenly the woman gave up. The paramedics were still working, but the woman sagged in Kate's arms.

"He's gone," she said. "I know it. This time he's gone."

Kate swam through darkness. She touched the hull of a sailboat, then swam on. She was deep undersea and had been swimming for miles. All she wanted to do was sleep, she thought. Then she saw it, the flash of a white face. Justin!

She swam hard, but the face disappeared. She couldn't find him, couldn't save him. No, wait! There! Justin! Her arms wrapped around him.

Her arms wrapped around a cold white fish.

He's gone, she knew it, this time he was gone.

"Kate, Kate, wake up. Come on now." His voice was gentle.

Kate opened her eyes and Tosh gazed down at her, his face full of concern. Another nightmare.

But the room was bright with sun now, the curtains blowing in.

"What time is it?"

"Nine o'clock."

"Nine o'clock! I'll be late for work!"

"Whoa!" He caught her and flattened her against the bed.

She lay there, stunned for a moment, staring up at him.

"Easy, girl," he said. Then he softly wiped away the tears on her face. "You're off today, remember?"

"I don't need off," she said. "I can handle this."

But he wouldn't let her up. "You handled it wonderfully. Even Luis said so. And Marta says he's not one to dish out compliments."

Kate closed her eyes. That was for sure. Luis

had come back to the beach yesterday to give her the news. The man had died. Coronary arrest, his third in eighteen months.

Kate didn't care if it was the thirtieth. Maybe if she had gotten to him sooner, maybe if she had whistled him in for a lecture ten minutes before, maybe if . . .

Luis had stared at her hard. It was a look that could subdue a great white shark. "I'm saying this once, so you better listen, Quinn. You did just what you should have done. You did good. Got it?"

She had nodded silently.

"By the way," he said, turning to leave, "my name is *Luis*."

Kate opened her eyes and looked into bright blue ones. *His* name was Tosh.

Luis and Tosh. Chelsea. Connor. Grace and David. Marta. Bo. Even Roan. These were the people in her life now, the people she needed to be strong and alive for. Justin was gone and it was time that she let him go.

And she would. But she had to sleep now; she was tired, so tired.

"Need to rest a little longer?" Tosh asked softly.

Kate nodded, then reached up and touched him on the mouth.

Tosh smiled. He leaned down and kissed her gently.

"Sleep now. I'll be here when you wake up. I'm here for you, Kate. I love you, Kate."

THIRTEEN

Chelsea squinted at the photograph once more. When Maurice, who owned Face Place, first told her where he kept the magnifying glass, she had thought her boss was kidding. No one would show you a blurry little snapshot with a head no bigger than the tip of your pinkie and ask you to create a portrait from it.

In the last week she had learned that Maurice had a great sense of humor, but he was rarely kidding. Perhaps that's what made him such a good caricaturist. He had started Face Place as a graduate with an art degree and no job. Twenty-five years later, he was still sitting in his narrow gallery off the boardwalk, seriously making fun of people through caricatures. Only now, he also employed three people as portrait artists and owned a similar setup in the Treasure Trove Mall.

At the boardwalk gallery Chelsea worked between Steve and Sophie. Steve, who went to the Maryland Institute of Art, was tall, black, and movie-star gorgeous. Sophie was an older, bleached-blond divorcée who liked to wear white boots. Steve had the training, Sophie had the touch, and Chelsea was learning from both of them. But neither could teach her how to create a good likeness from a quarter-inch blur.

While studying the photo, it occurred to Chelsea that her client was probably in love with the woman in the picture. He probably saw all kinds of beauty in this badly processed film and string bean of a woman. He saw what no one else could see, even if the woman had been there in person. Chelsea began to question him. What made him fall in love with her? What were her eyes like? How about her smile?

She discovered that it was the mysterious hazel of the woman's eyes that captured his heart, and the sweetness of her mouth, even when she wasn't smiling. Improvising, Chelsea drew from this lover's vision as much as from the woman's photograph. She was rewarded with a huge tip.

"You earned that one," Maurice said. "Take a break, Chelsea. Then you next, Steve. We got a few more hours before we send these weekenders home."

Chelsea nodded and began to clean off her hands.

"Six o'clock quitting time," Steve said. "How I love Sundays in June!"

"Mmm," Chelsea murmured. She would love them too, if she had something to do. But Kate would be with Tosh this evening and David was taking out Grace to celebrate her first week in business. As for Marta, she had chattered all the way through the eleven o'clock news last night. Marta, of all people, had come extremely close to saying some girlish and silly things—and all because Dracula called saying he wanted to see her Sunday night. So.

So, thought Chelsea, maybe Bo was free this evening to teach her a few skateboard tricks. She pictured herself lying in several pieces on the driveway.

"So," he said, "do you have plans?"

"I'm sorry?"

"I know it's kind of last minute," Steve went on apologetically. He had a deep voice, the warmest brown eyes in the world, and a mouth she'd love to draw, strong and sensitive. "Please don't feel as if you have to say yes."

"I don't think I heard the question," said Chelsea.

"I asked if you'd like to join me for dinner tonight at my condo—my parents' condo. They come down most weekends. Before they return to Washington tonight, we're having some crabs. Would—would you like to come?"

Chelsea blinked. Steve was asking her out.

No, Steve was asking her over. No big deal.

Well, actually, he was asking her to his place—which *could* be a big deal. But she would be eating with his family—no big deal. She would leave when his parents left.

Why should she leave when his parents left? Here was this sensitive, talented hunk of a guy asking her to his place. Why should she make an early exit—so she could check in with Connor? Go for it, she told herself. After all, she was separated. She was alone. She was a woman in search of her own heart—*My Condo Love*, she thought, imagining Steve and her on a book cover, with gold embossed print, of course.

"That's okay, Chelsea. You don't have to think of a way to say no nicely. I understand. Maybe some other time."

"Some other time," she echoed. "I would really, really I would like to . . . to meet your family some other time."

Steve nodded, and she made a quick escape past Maurice and onto the crowded boardwalk.

Wimp, she chided herself. Now what did she have to look forward to? A whole night alone to think about Connor.

She tried to focus on the people around her and enjoy twenty minutes of Sunday afternoon on the boards. A baby stroller rumbled along next to her. The train rolled past, looking like a huge and friendly caterpillar. People lined up at Dilly's, buying rainbows of taffy. In cavernous video arcades, twelve-year-old boys destroyed villains and conquered star systems. Twelve-year-old girls stretched out in the sun and waited for the boys to grow up.

Maybe Bo would let her treat him to a movie. Maybe Roan could use a friendly ear and an evening out. Chelsea had felt sorry for the girl ever since she had told her how hard it was to be the oldest of five kids with alcoholic parents.

Maybe she should have said yes to Steve.

The guy was incredibly attractive. Sophie and she had agreed that half the women who sat for him didn't care diddly about their portraits; they just wanted an excuse to stare at him, and they loved having him look back at them with undivided attention.

How wrong was it to enjoy an evening with such a charming guy and his family, especially since Connor said there were no rules to keep?

And yet, in her heart, Chelsea felt certain that Connor had set up his own rules for himself. Oh, he loved to scoff at requirements and regulations, social codes and traditional values; he enjoyed a reputation as an eccentric and free spirit. But he ordered his own private world very carefully. He had his own hard rules for himself and intense feelings about what he owed people.

Chelsea knew that for all that he said about

no rules and total freedom, he would not be rushing out to date other women. So, she had no heart for other guys. That was that. At least for now, she thought.

She bought herself a double-dip peach swirl ice-cream cone and sat on a bench to watch more of Ocean City's never-ending parade. She wished Connor were there to give his usual wry commentary. Instead, a rather grim-looking fellow in a pale blue shirt and dark blue slacks sat down next to her. He, too, watched the parade, but he didn't seem to be enjoying it.

The next moment, neither was Chelsea. Coming down the boardwalk, totally unaware of her presence, was Connor, and with him, talking to him, touching him, was another woman. Snow White. At least she resembled Snow White, with her long black hair, ivory skin, and bright cherry smile. All she needed were birds perched on her hands.

She and Connor were talking and laughing as if they had known each other forever.

Keep calm, Chelsea told herself. They're just talking, they're just laughing, they're just friends. I am calm. I am thoroughly and metaphysically calm. I am in complete control.

Then she jumped up and slammed down her ice-cream cone.

"What the—"

She had forgotten all about the man in the

blue slacks next to her. Pink swirl glopped down his pants and puddled on his shiny black shoes. He stared up at Chelsea in disbelief.

Out of the corner of her eye she saw Connor watching her.

Then she saw him put his arm around Snow White and pull her close to him, turning her face away from Chelsea. Behind them was a narrow space that ran between two buildings. Chelsea watched as Connor and the girl hurried down the passageway like two mice caught playing by a plump old cat.

"I'm glad you changed your mind, Chelsea," Steve said, still sounding surprised by her sudden reversal.

"I'm looking forward to this," she replied. She was scanning the sidewalks as Steve drove north to Grace's. At any moment she expected to see Connor walking arm in arm with Snow White.

"I came straight from Columbia to O.C. this year," Chelsea added, "and I've missed Sunday dinners with the family."

Steve smiled and seemed to relax a little. There was something utterly charming about a hunk of a guy who was shy around a girl. "I figured you were the kind of woman who would understand—understand my situation and the way my family thinks."

"How do they think?"

His eyebrows drew together. "Well, my mother, who works for the Justice Department, is a staunch conservative in politics. But on family matters she generally votes liberal. My dad, on the other hand, is a liberal Democratic congressman, but a hard-line—maybe I should say a hard-*head*—conservative when it comes to goals and expectations for his children."

"We'll get along just fine," Chelsea assured him. "I'll pretend I'm talking to my parents."

He squeezed her hand. "Thanks. I knew you'd be cool about this."

"Turn here," she said, pointing to Grace's driveway. "Home sweet home."

As soon as Steve pulled the key out of the ignition, he hopped out of the car and hurried around to get Chelsea's door. Chelsea hoped Connor happened to look out his window then. He could use a few lessons in chivalry.

"This place is impressive," Steve remarked as Chelsea unlocked the front door.

"The mix of people who live here is even more remarkable," she replied. "You never know who Grace is going to take in next. Anybody home?" she called.

She heard a drawer roll shut in the kitchen and two sets of footsteps.

"Hullo."

Chelsea stared. It was that girl! The fairy-tale

180

beauty Connor had been strolling down the boardwalk with.

"You must be Chelsea," said the girl.

Chelsea nodded.

"I'm—"

"Snow White," thought Chelsea.

Tosh blinked and Steve coughed quietly.

Realizing she had spoken the words aloud, Chelsea put her hand over her mouth.

The girl's eyes twinkled. "Actually, I'm Colleen," she said.

"Fresh from the old country," Tosh informed Chelsea.

Just what I need, thought Chelsea, another Irish girl. Another woman from Connor's past. "And are you freshly pregnant too?" she blurted. "Or have you brought a child with you?"

This time Steve's discreet cough sounded more like choking. He's having second thoughts, thought Chelsea. He's not so sure I'm the right woman to bring home to Mom and Dad.

But she couldn't worry about that, not with this beautiful Irish girl standing before her, challenging her. Chelsea had been through this routine last year with one of Connor's old girlfriends. Molly had come with a child, conveniently named Connie, seeking support and a green card. Blood tests had proved the child wasn't Connor's, but what was to prevent others from trying?

"Only Molly would try something like that," Colleen replied.

Chelsea asked. "You know Molly?"

"Quite well," the girl said. "Molly could sniff them out, she could, the really decent lads who would take responsibility and show some kindness. She had Connor figured out. She just didn't count on you." Colleen smiled a dazzling smile.

Chelsea nodded. So there was no child. Still, she didn't like the guilty manner in which Connor had hurried away with this beauty.

"And this is?" Colleen asked, looking up at Steve.

"Uh, Steve. We work together."

"Lovely to meet you, Steve."

He took her hand. Tosh eyed Steve up and down, then turned to Chelsea, raising an eyebrow. She ignored his silent question.

Steve, being a man of manners, introduced himself to Tosh and shook his hand.

"So who are you sleeping with?" Chelsea asked Colleen. "I mean, which room are you staying in?"

"Well, I was living with Irish pals before, but we had to scatter when the Immies showed up. Grace offered me the sofa in the living room, but I have an American friend living a few blocks away. So I'll stay with her a bit. Of course, my evacuation route leads to

Connor's apartment first, then Landfall."

"Great," said Chelsea. To Connor's apartment first. Not yours and Connor's, just Connor's. So she must know about their separation. And surely she realized that nothing was more appealing to a guy than a beautiful girl in need of rescue.

"Well, I'm going upstairs to freshen up," Chelsea said. And to beat my pillow till it looks like a croaked chicken, she thought.

"Chelsea," Colleen called after her. "I didn't see you today on the boardwalk."

Chelsea swung around. So, now they were getting to what really mattered.

"But Connor did, of course," Colleen added.

"I know Connor did," Chelsea said, keeping her voice as even as possible.

"Lucky for me," Colleen went on. "I have you to thank as much as Connor. If Connor hadn't spotted you in the crowd, he wouldn't have spotted the Immy sitting next to you."

"The—Immigration officer?" Chelsea said softly, and thought about the man in the blue pants, the pants she had decorated with large globs of peach swirl.

"It was wonderfully quick thinking on your part," Colleen went on. "Startling that Immy as you did, you gave me enough time to get away. I owe you a large ice cream."

Chelsea rubbed her head, which was starting

to hurt. "It's on me," she said. "Consider it part of your American welcome."

Then she left Tosh, Colleen, and Steve to get to know one another. She needed time in the bathroom, a lot of time to think about what she was going to tell Steve and to scrape the egg— make that ice cream—off her face.

FOURTEEN

"Should I try another bathroom, Chelsea, or are you planning to come out before Labor Day?"

Chelsea opened the door and Kate waved a makeup case at her. "Lighting is bad in my room. And I, well, I've got a hot date." She gave a lopsided smile.

"So do I," said Chelsea.

Kate looked surprised; then she gripped Chelsea's arm. "I'm so glad to hear that!"

"You are?" Chelsea moved over so Kate could share the mirror with her. "I thought maybe you wouldn't approve."

"Because I once said you were marrying too young?" Kate studied Chelsea's reflection, then leaned toward her own. "Chels, you know I've been wrong about things more than once in my life. Besides, I approve of anything that makes you happier than you've been this week."

"Well, good," said Chelsea. "Because my date isn't with Connor."

Kate's hand jumped. Her mascara brush painted an extra set of lashes on her cheek.

Chelsea kept her eyes on her own reflection. "It was Connor's idea, really," she said. "Connor was the one who brought up the matter of dating other people. He was the one who said he didn't want any rules."

Chelsea began to color her lips. Red, cherry red. Mirror, mirror on the wall, she thought.

"Well, maybe he did," Kate replied, "but the day I see Connor with another woman—"

"Maybe you ought to meet our newest house-guest before drawing any hasty conclusions," said Chelsea.

Kate frowned.

"And speaking of seeing other people," Chelsea went on, "you're not exactly in widow's weeds." She eyed Kate's sexy underwear. "Though perhaps that's why you are wearing your *black* peekaboo camisole."

Kate's cheeks flushed and she turned away quickly.

Chelsea instantly regretted her words. "I'm sorry, Kate. I'm sorry. I'm just so mixed up. I guess I'm trying to get you mixed up with me. Don't let me."

Kate didn't reply.

"*You* know what you need," Chelsea continued. "And I know you deserve a new love. We both know that Tosh has been good to you."

"He has been wonderful," Kate replied, dipping her finger in the cold cream that Chelsea offered her, wiping the mascara off her cheek.

"So go for it," Chelsea encouraged softly.

"I am."

Chelsea nodded, then stared at her painted mouth. It looked like she had stuck a strawberry on it.

Kate turned to face her directly. "And how about you, Chels? Seems to me you deserve to find the kind of love that is right for you."

Chelsea shook her head slowly. "I thought Connor was right for me. I mean, how could I love so much someone who isn't right for me?" Her hands dropped to her sides. "I've made such a mess of things, Kate. And I'm so afraid that while I'm straightening out my mess, I'm hurting Connor. Do you know how hurting him would make me feel?"

Kate thought about Tosh. "I do," she said.

"But you aren't hurting anybody, Kate. I mean, Justin is gone, you've mourned him, you're free, and now there's Tosh—"

"It's no different," Kate said. "Anytime you reach out, anytime you try love, you risk hurting someone else as well as yourself. There's no getting around that, for me or you. And there's no getting around the fact that everyone makes mistakes."

Chelsea bit her lip.

"You still deserve the chance to find happiness, Chelsea. You and Connor each deserve to find it."

Chelsea looked up and saw her friend's moist eyes. Kate knew how painful it could be.

"Now stop that!" Chelsea said, blinking back her own tears. "Stop it, and blink carefully. Otherwise you're going to have ditto marks all the way down your cheeks."

Then she reached over and wiped Kate's streaky mascara. "Love's messy, isn't it?"

"Sure is."

They both turned back to the mirror again.

"So who is he?" asked Kate. "Who is this hot date?"

"Steve, from work. I mentioned him before."

"The sensitive hunk? Don't leave till I get a good look at him."

Chelsea smiled.

"Two artistes on the town," Kate continued. "What are you going to wear?"

"My one and only ordinary white shirt—and a lot of perfume, since it needs washing. For our first date, we're eating with the conservative parent corps."

"Want to borrow something?" Kate offered. "My blue-and-white stripe is in the dryer."

"Bless you! Can I lend you my peacock feather earrings, or perhaps my sequined socks?"

Kate laughed. "I saw your short, swishy skirt hanging up to dry—"

"It's yours!" said Chelsea. "And may the wind be blowing tonight!"

They laughed, then ran for their robes and crept down the stairs. Kate glanced around the corner. "All clear." Together they sprinted for the laundry room.

Its door was closed. Inside they heard some singing and lots of muffled laughter. "What the heck?" Chelsea said, leaning against the door, putting her ear to it. A second later, it opened.

"Yo!" said Chelsea tumbling inward. She landed in Marta's lap and the two of them flew backward, rolling past the washer and dryer, bulldozing a pile beneath the laundry chute. Yelps of laughter escaped Grace. Kate hurried in, and Grace closed the door behind her.

"What are you ladies up to?" Kate asked.

Marta wiped her laughing eyes. "Just talking," she said.

"She's delirious," said Grace. "I came in to get my dress and found her folding laundry and singing 'I Feel Pretty.'"

Kate and Chelsea looked at each other, then sang out, "Oh so pretty!"

Marta joined them: "I feel pretty and witty and bright!"

Grace rolled her eyes. "Just what I need in my house, the cast from a Broadway musical."

189

"Look at it this way," Chelsea replied. "Most of those old musicals ended happily ever after."

"I don't think this one did," Kate reminded her.

"Ours will," asserted Marta.

"All right," Grace said with a shrug. "I feel pretty, oh so pretty—"

"Flat, flat, flat!" exclaimed Chelsea. "Grace! I never knew, you can't sing worth a darn!"

Everyone laughed, and Marta sang on. The others joined her, mixing up the lines and verses. Kate danced with a laundry basket. Chelsea swung bras. Their voices grew louder and louder.

Then the doorbell rang.

"Shh! Shh!"

"Who is it?"

"David. He's always early!"

"Maybe it's Dominic."

Kate cracked open the laundry door, and the girls crowded close.

"Why, hello, Connor," said Tosh.

Chelsea put her hand over her mouth and glanced at Kate.

"Do you—do you want to come in?" Tosh asked politely.

"And meet Steve?" Chelsea added softly.

"Thanks, no," Connor replied. "Just tell Colleen that the way is clear and her friend is waiting for her."

"Will do."

Chelsea breathed a sigh of relief.

"Oh, and one more thing—"

He saw, thought Chelsea.

"Yes?" said Tosh.

"You might tell the ladies of Landfall that there is an audience forming out here on the street, and they're crying for more." Connor raised his voice. "Go away, guys. Shoo! Shoo!"

Tosh laughed. "Anything else?"

"Actually, yes. Would you tell Chelsea I saw her today and I wanted her to know—no, never mind. It doesn't matter. See you later."

"Later," Tosh replied.

Too late, thought Chelsea.

"Is this okay?" Dominic asked Marta.

For an evening out with him, Tina Wina Tacos would have been okay.

"This is where Mr. DiPaola said I should take you," he added.

They gazed up at The Claw restaurant. Its large picture windows, which faced the board-walk, glimmered with the haloed light of candles and softly lit lamps.

"Mr. DiPaola?" she repeated, amused. "You discussed restaurants the night you brought him into the clinic?"

"No, we discussed restaurants at breakfast yesterday. Or maybe it was dinner Wednesday night, I can't remember. Both times he served jelly toast and cold Spaghetti-Os."

Marta smiled to herself. Now she knew why the old man hadn't been around to the clinic looking for attention. He had found himself a friend.

She turned her gaze on Dominic. He was tugging on the neck of what must have been his one good shirt. The tie looked as if it had been borrowed from Mr. DiPaola. She lightly touched his other hand, which was resting on her chair. "Mr. DiPaola advised you well. This is lovely."

Though the restaurant wasn't crowded on a Sunday night, Dominic had called earlier to request a seat by the window. The cozy table for two with a candle, fresh flowers, sparkling glassware, and a little "Reserved" sign was waiting for them.

Marta opened her menu, trying to act like a woman who had done this kind of thing before. She *had* done this kind of thing before! With Alec, who had lots of good shirts, was used to wearing ties, and would never take the dining advice of a man who liked cold Spaghetti-Os.

Slowly she lowered her menu for a peek at Dominic in the candlelight.

His menu was already lowered. They looked at each other, then quickly raised their menus again.

After quite a bit of discussion from either side of the paper wall, she ordered stuffed flounder, and he, soft-shell crabs.

"Mr. DiPaola suggested them," Dominic added as explanation for his choice.

"Well, I had no idea that Mr. DiPaola was such a man about town," Marta replied, her eyes twinkling. "I assume he told you how soft crabs are served."

Dominic shook his head, then shrugged. "I'd enjoy anything tonight."

"We'll see," she said with a smile, then asked, "How's your job going?"

He told her about all the people who worked at the amusement pier. It fascinated Marta that a guy who was so secretive about himself could so enjoy relating the details of everybody else's life. He also described the people he took on tour through Horror Hall.

The day before, a kid had smuggled a small dog into the haunted house. It had gotten loose and trotted across the bed of nails—rubber nails that looked convincingly sharp. A large woman on the tour fainted dead away. Dominic gallantly rushed to her side to revive her. He forgot about one thing, however: his costume. The woman woke to find a vampire bending over her, and immediately passed out again.

Meanwhile another tour had caught up with his. The two tours got mixed up, people were wandering every whichway, and the dog was racing around the house through invisible doors, tripping tourists, knocking down props. For ten minutes the place was filled with shrieks and general confusion. Word got around, and business was brisk after that.

The way he told the story, mimicking the expressions of the people running around the spook house, made Marta laugh and laugh. She started to hiccup, and he quickly offered her a water glass. Her lips brushed his fingers, then she took a long drink, letting him hold the glass for her. "Thank you."

He set the glass down and pulled back his hand somewhat reluctantly.

"Flounder," said the waitress, seizing the moment to slip between them, "and soft-shells."

Dominic stared down at his plate. He looked up at the waitress, then over at Marta.

"Enjoy your meals," said the waitress. "Is there anything else I can bring for you right now?"

Marta shook her head. "Thank you," she said for the speechless Dominic.

The young woman departed. Dominic was still staring at his plate. He pointed at the crusty brown strings that poked out between two slices of toasted bread. "What are those things?"

"What things?" asked Marta.

"Those things that look like claws."

"Claws."

Dominic nudged one of them as if he expected it to move. "How do I remove the claws?"

"You bite them."

"I bite them and spit them out?"

"You bite them and chew them up."

"Oh."

She reached over, plucked off a claw and popped it into her mouth. "Mmm."

Dominic looked uncertain. He lifted the lid of his sandwich. "The whole crab is there, shell and all!"

"Not the whole crab," she corrected him. "They scooped out the lungs for you, and snipped off the eyes and mouth."

Dominic's own mouth twitched.

"They really are good, Dominic." She felt the laughter bubbling up, bubbling through her, the way the heat ran through her in one of their more romantic moments.

"In a fancy place like this, some people use a knife and fork," she continued. "But I'd just pick him up like a sandwich and chew away."

"Him," Dominic repeated. "He's probably longing to jump in my water glass." He took a breath, lifted the sandwich to his mouth, and bit. Crab juice squirted across the table at her.

Marta threw back her head and laughed. Several patrons turned around. Dominic looked embarrassed.

"I wish this dinner was as much fun for you as it is for me," she said. She leaned forward, smiling into his eyes, and he relaxed a little.

By the time Dominic had finished both crabs,

he had decided it was the best seafood he'd ever had.

Marta let him pay the bill and waited till they got outside to hand him money for her half of the dinner. She was breaking rules she had set for herself long ago. Rule number one: If a guy wants to treat you to dinner, let him; then you treat him the next time. Rule number two: If you're going Dutch, pay at the table; don't massage that tender male ego by letting him look like he's paying, then contributing later.

But Marta had been breaking her own rules since she met Dominic. She continually surprised herself. Good old in-your-face Marta kept looking beyond herself, at his face, trying to read and understand what he needed and wanted. Maybe she would regret it, she thought, but she wasn't going to turn back now. The mystery of Dominic drew her on.

"What's that for?" he asked as she tried to put the money in his hand.

"Dinner."

"Thanks. But I was treating," he said.

"Thanks, but we were going Dutch," she replied.

"No," he said.

"Yes," she insisted.

"When I invite a girl out, I treat."

"And what do you expect in return?" she asked, a little piqued.

"From you, nothing."

From *her*, nothing? Marta's eyelids flew wide. "If there is one thing I can't stand," she said, "it's a macho, Latino male—"

He stared down at her.

"—a macho, Latino male who acts nice to girls in wheelchairs and lonely old men!" she blurted, afraid that it was true.

His black eyes flashed at her. She could see some kind of dark emotion moving through him, emotion he wanted to hide. Marta bit her lip. Her own anger began to ebb, but she was tempted to egg him on.

Why would she do such a stupid thing? she wondered. Playing with fire, wasn't that how Grace described getting involved with men of mystery? You never knew what you'd find out. But the dark river that ran through Dominic drew Marta on, and she was tempted to force it to the surface, using anger if necessary.

Then Dominic turned away from her. He held out his hand so that she could lay the money in it. He pocketed it. Her chance to learn more was gone.

She leaned forward, trying to see his face. "Dominic, I would like to—Dominic?"

"Yes?" he said at last.

"I'd enjoy a ride down the boardwalk after dinner," she said quietly. "If you want to walk along, that would be nice, but I understand if you'd like to go home now."

He was silent for a moment, then said, "I'd like to walk with you."

"Good."

They moved along side by side, both staring straight ahead. There were few people on the boardwalk that night, mostly locals, and only the largest shops remained lit. When they reached the pier, its gate was open for the night fishermen, but its rides were dark, collapsed like umbrellas.

"Which way?" he asked her. "The pier or straight ahead?"

"I love the pier. The very end," she said.

When they came to the spook house, they paused, gazing up at its plasterboard front, crooked gables, and motionless bats. It looked more eerie in the pale moonlight than it did bathed in its lurid red light with the soundtrack going.

"Is this the first job you've had since you left L.A.?" Marta asked.

"No. I picked up some temporary work to pay my way across the country."

"Why did you come east?"

"Why did you?" he asked quickly.

"I suppose because my dad wanted to be as far away as we could get from L.A."

He nodded.

"But don't you think it's a coincidence," she went on, "or some kind of strange fate, that two people who once lived in the same neighborhood and went to the same school, yet never met, would travel three thousand miles, and seven years later meet one weekend in a little beach town crowded in with a hundred thousand other people?"

"Perhaps it was all some kind of fate," he replied, then moved ahead of her.

She followed him past the last ride to the T-shaped end of the pier. It was dark, except for the wash of moonlight and the yellow lanterns of two fishermen. The fishermen leaned against the rail, trailing their lines far below into the sea.

"Why do you like it here?" Dominic asked. "Is it the view of the town?"

The boardwalk lay behind them. On a sunny day it looked like a colorful strip from a game board; at night it was a sparkling bracelet laid out on black velvet. But that wasn't what drew Marta. She liked being this far out, where the ocean heaved against the pilings, too deep to break. She liked feeling its power and watching it swirl around the spindly legs of the pier.

"No, I rarely look behind me." She rolled herself over to the railing. "Would you lift me up, please, so I can sit on the top rail? It's difficult to see through this fencing."

"What if you fall?" he asked.

"You won't let me," she said, holding her arms up to him.

He hesitated.

"I trust you, Dominic."

His face looked white in the moonlight, but he lifted her up. Setting her on the rail, he held on to her for dear life.

"I feel like a bird up here," she said, "hovering above the churning sea—maybe an osprey, making my nest over the water."

She felt his face very close to hers. His eyes searched hers for something. She wished she knew what he sought.

"Birds are my inspiration," she said. "Legs are useful to them—as they would be to me—but we can both fly without them." Dominic moved his head then, and she thought he wanted to move away from her. But his face swung back, his lips very close to hers. She could feel him quivering.

Then his lips touched hers. He was kissing her and holding her close. He held her so close, his need, his fear, his want ran through her hot and cold, till both of them were shivering, both of them reaching, both clinging to each other, high above a long drop at the end of a very long pier.

FIFTEEN

"You told me to put on my sparkles," Grace said.

David had risen slowly from the deck chair and was staring at her, amazed.

"Should I change?"

"God, no!" he said, and then more softly, "Let's go."

Grace waved good-bye to Tosh, who was still waiting for Kate.

"I think we should take my car," she said when she and David got outside. The slit in her skirt ran most of the way up her leg, so perhaps she could straddle the seat of his motorcycle and the two of them could roar off into the sunset; but sequins and long drop earrings should travel by coach, she thought.

"Is everything okay, David? You have a funny look on your face."

He was gazing at her next to the BMW, his

head cocked to one side. "You know, you look like a car ad."

"Why, you old sweet talker," Grace said, shaking her head.

David moved close to her. "When am I going to get used to you?"

"Used to me?"

"You still startle me, Grace, how beautiful you are."

She gazed up at him. *He* still startled her. No one had ever loved her the way he did. No one had known her so well and still, somehow, loved her.

She kissed him lightly.

He responded with a long deep kiss, then another and another.

She came up for breath. "Pardon me while I throw myself across the car hood."

He laughed low in his throat. "They don't do shots like that for classy cars, or classy ladies."

"Just as well," she said briskly. "We should get going. What time is our reservation?"

"Ten o'clock."

"Ten o'clock!" she echoed with surprise.

"I brought snacks," David said.

"What did you plan to do between now and then, besides eat Dorritos?"

"Fly," he said. "Fly there, I mean."

"Where?"

"To our reservation in Washington. And we

202

don't serve Doritos on Air David," he added. "Smoked salmon, gorgonzola cheese, the finest rice crackers, and Perrier."

"What a romantic you are!"

"One of us has to be," he said with a smile, then got into the car.

They drove to the airfield north of Ocean City where she had first met David. It had been a while since Grace had been up in his Cessna. He had taught her well, however—well enough for her to have made her first solo flight last summer. Sequins or no sequins, she put on the headset, checked the gauges, and waited for the rush.

Grace loved the feel of the small plane's acceleration. "Pedal faster!" she cried. Then the engine roared and the scrub pines became a line painted by a wet green brush. The white pavement rushed toward them. It came faster and faster, till the earth finally let them go. There was the sudden lift. They were up and circling over the ocean, then heading west into the melting sunscape.

She and David could talk through the headset, but they said little. They were enjoying the darkening land, the winking of farmhouse lights here and there. They crossed over a highway of departing shore traffic—its line of cars looking like a string of chaser lights—then the purple silk of the Chesapeake Bay. It was nearly dark when they circled over Washington.

"Oz," David said into the headphones.

"Disney World," she replied, looking down at the floodlit buildings and monuments.

They parked at an airfield in Virginia and took a taxi into the city. They were early for their reservation, and David asked the driver to loop around some of the sites.

"I feel a thousand miles from home," Grace said.

"It's good for you," David replied, putting his arm around her. "Since you arrived back in April, you've had a lot to handle, Grace. You still have a lot."

She laid her head back against his shoulder. "I think things are settling down now." Ahead of them the streetlamps made a starry bridge over the Potomac River and into the heart of the city. "Really," she continued, "it's only Roan I'm concerned about, though at least I understand her better."

"What are you going to do about her?" David asked.

Grace had been wondering that all week.

"I don't know. She can't stay with me forever. She's a minor—she shouldn't be with me at all. But how can I send a kid back to a mother who can't keep her hot run of boyfriends away from her daughter?"

David frowned. "Say that again?"

"Roan and I had a talk this week, when I hauled her home at three a.m. It seems her mother has had a lot of boyfriends, and the bastards get two for the price of one."

David sucked in his breath.

"Pretty grim, huh?"

"Strange," David said thoughtfully.

"I'm afraid not," Grace replied, staring out the window. "That kind of thing happens more often than you'd think."

"That's not what I meant. She told Tosh she lived with her father."

"What?" Grace turned so quickly, her purse slipped off her lap.

"Roan told Tosh she lived with her father."

"Well . . . Tosh must have gotten the story mixed up," Grace said.

"With her father and stepmother," David continued, "a wicked stepmother, of course, who made her life miserable."

Grace retrieved her purse and played with the black beads that fringed it. "Maybe Roan was embarrassed to tell him the true story," she suggested.

"Maybe," David replied, "but I think you should be careful. You really know nothing about her, Grace."

"No, but I know myself," she said confidently.

"Don't confuse yourself with Roan—"

"I didn't say I—"

"And don't trust her too quickly," he added.

"I can't pull out on her, David!"

205

"I'm not suggesting you do." He stroked her hand. "Just keep in mind that you can't save her, either."

"Certainly not in a week," Grace said.

"And not in a summer, maybe not in a lifetime."

"Spoken by a man who knows my track record," Grace replied.

"What do you mean by that?" David asked sharply. "You're not referring to Justin and your mother?"

Grace didn't answer him right away. They were driving past the museums that lined the National Mall; the tall trees lining the avenue arched above them with spray after spray of fresh summer leaves. It was going to be strange, greeting each new season without her mother and Justin.

"I wasn't referring to Justin," Grace said at last. "I couldn't have rescued him, I realize that now. Besides, things were good between us when he died. I've made my peace with him."

"And your mother?"

"My mother." She shook her head. "This belonged to her." Grace held up her right hand so he could see the ring with its star sapphire.

"I don't think I've seen that before," he said.

"I kept her jewelry. This is the first time I've worn any of it. When I was a kid, I picked this ring out for her. I was fascinated by the milky blue stone and the way it splintered light into a star. I don't think she liked it all that much, but

206

she wore it because I liked it. At least, she did when I was younger. If only I could have stayed young in the way I saw her, more childlike and accepting, like Bo."

"That's not realistic, or helpful, Grace."

"And what I did was? When I came back, as soon as we were together again, I screamed and screamed at her. I said horrible things. Why? I was getting my own life together. She wasn't hurting me anymore. Why couldn't I have made peace with her?"

"Because she *was* hurting you. She was a drunk bent on destroying someone you loved very much—herself."

Tears ran down Grace's cheeks. "It's so much easier for you to say that I . . . I loved her."

"Give yourself time, Grace. It hasn't been that long."

She nodded, and they rode quietly the rest of the way, her damp face pressed against him.

"Maybe I better find a ladies' room," she said when they pulled up in front of the restaurant. "Did I do major damage to my makeup?"

"No, but it's always worth checking out the bathrooms in places like these."

She laughed a little.

They ate with other late diners, then walked through Georgetown, along the streets of narrow row houses and quaint restaurants and shops. There were other couples strolling, friends and lovers waiting for the late moon to come up.

It was very late when they took a cab back to the airfield. They flew home beneath a brilliant night sky and above lavender and orange clusters of lights.

"I like flying at night," Grace said. "There are stars above you and stars below."

"Lots of stars to wish on," said David.

Grace looked down at her ring. "And to travel by."

SIXTEEN

"Chelsea, this is my dad."

"Hello, Mr. Hunt."

"Call me Hamilton," said Steve's father. "Nice to meet you, Chelsea."

"And my mother," said Steve.

Now this, thought Chelsea, was a woman who knew how to dress—casual but carefully coordinated, African-American but definitely Washingtonian. How did she do it?

"Welcome, Chelsea," said the politically correct dresser. "I'm Susannah."

"This is Kenneth."

"Older brother?" Chelsea guessed.

"My father's chief aide," Steve replied. "And Audrey and Andy Powell."

Well, they weren't relatives; they were white.

"Strong backers of my father," Steve whispered to her after the shaking of hands.

"Contributed a bundle to his last campaign."

"I thought this was going to be a family dinner," Chelsea whispered back.

"They are family. Political family."

Chelsea nodded, then noticed the congressman watching her and Steve. She was surprised by his rather obvious expression of approval. Did he judge everyone that quickly? She felt guilty. What if he knew his son was interested in a married woman?

Steve laid his hand on Chelsea's back. "Let me give you a tour of the place," he said.

The condo was two stories of a low-rise building facing the beach. It had beige carpet and beige leather chairs (plus a beige microwave, beige telephone, beige toilet, tasteful beige trash cans). Just about anything that wasn't beige had a thin green stripe in it or was made of glass. It would be easy to buy these people a house gift, Chelsea thought.

But Steve's room was different: it was alive with color. Chelsea stood in the middle of it and slowly turned around. Though the room was exceptionally neat, the images on the wall shattered any sense of a life that was ordered and tranquil. Most of the paintings were of birds—a gull caught in fishing line, quails thrashing inside a net, a bright bird with a bloody breast pressed against the bars of a cage. They were painted in realistic detail, and their pain was something she couldn't turn away from.

Steve remained silent, giving Chelsea time to look.

"Harsh," she said softly.

He gave a nervous laugh. "I'll take that as a compliment."

"Did you bring me here because you wanted me to weep?"

"Two compliments, I think."

"Maybe I'd better get your autograph now, before the world discovers you. Maybe I'd better get my portrait done, so I can have an original Steven Hunt. Though your portraits aren't anything like this."

"If I were to paint you, Chelsea, it wouldn't turn out like one of our boardwalk pictures. You might not even recognize yourself, at least at first."

"How would you paint me?"

He thought for a moment. "As a strong and colorful bird with a gold ring around her neck."

She puzzled over that. "Is the ring something beautiful, or is it an animal collar, something to attach a leash to?"

"Exactly," he replied.

Perhaps, thought Chelsea, he did know her situation. Perhaps he had noticed that her wide gold band was missing from the collection of rings she usually wore on the job.

Chelsea started wondering who his other birds were, the ones caught in fishing line, a net, and a cage. Her eyes swept around the room again.

"Who's this?" she asked, noticing a photo on Steve's bureau. It was the only one of the group in black and white, and the young man's expression drew you immediately toward him. "Now, I could draw a portrait from *this* photo!" she exclaimed. "What a face! He's not just smiling, he knows something—and maybe he'll share this wonderful secret with you and maybe he won't."

Steve laughed softly, then said, "I took that picture."

"Who is it?"

"Frank. He's a student at the Institute too," Steve said. Then he took a manila envelope out of his top drawer. "Do you want to see some other pictures I've taken of him?"

"Sure."

Chelsea sat down on the bed and Steve sat down close to her, laying the envelope on both of their laps. She was aware that when they had entered his bedroom, he'd shut the door behind them. She had noticed it because, at the Lennox house, you didn't go into the bedroom with someone of the opposite sex and close the door. If you tried it, Chelsea's father would walk right in behind you.

Which is why she jumped about a foot in the

air when someone thumped loudly on Steve's door. Hamilton Hunt called, "Soup's on!" but he didn't presume to open the door and he didn't wait for an answer.

Steve set the envelope aside and lightly touched Chelsea's hand. "You have nothing to worry about. My dad likes women with beauty and brains."

By the time they joined the others, everyone was slurping away. The glass dining-room table had been moved to the side, and a long folding table was set up and covered with newspapers. Steve steered Chelsea to a seat next to a girl that had to be his sister. She was quite slender, but had the same high cheekbones and beautiful eyes.

"I'm Judith," she said, taking in the details of Chelsea with undisguised curiosity. She even checked her left hand!

"Judith is on the same train line as you, Chelsea," he said, slipping in next to her. "She goes to Princeton."

"Do I understand correctly that you attend Columbia?" Hamilton called from the other end of the table.

He had been in the middle of a conversation with Kenneth, the aide, but Chelsea figured that a successful congressman was used to following several dialogues at once.

"Yes, sir."

"And you're an art student?" asked Susannah.

"Yes, ma'am."

"A polite one," observed Kenneth.

Chelsea wondered if he always sounded sarcastic.

"How do you like Columbia?" Susannah asked.

"I love it."

Hamilton leaned forward. "As an artist, do you find it worthwhile to be in a high-quality university with an excellent art department, rather than some art school?"

"Oh, yes! Our instructors are terrific and—" Suddenly she realized where this conversation was going. She remembered too late that Steve's parents didn't like the fact that their son was attending "some art school."

"Well, the studio instructors are pretty good," she said. "And besides, I wasn't as *fortunate* as Steve. I wasn't given any choice in schools." She saw Susannah nod, and felt as if she had scored with at least one parent on behalf of Steve. Perhaps she should have quit while she was ahead, but she felt compelled to go on. "My father didn't think about what would be best for me as an artist. He was so set on Columbia that even when Connor—"

She caught herself.

"Connor?"

"My . . . brother, Connor. Even when he—"

He what? What terrible, yet politically correct

214

thing could this fictitious brother have done to provoke her father's ire at Columbia?

"Ran away with his political-science professor—"

"Really!" said Audrey and Andy Powell. They were interested now.

"Well, not a professor, actually, a teaching assistant. Tosh."

"Connor ran away with Tosh?" Steve asked, his eyes growing round.

Chelsea had completely forgotten that the guys had met back at the house.

"Toshita," she said quickly. "Tosh is short for Toshita."

This was getting out of control.

"Well, that certainly is interesting," Kenneth said with barely hidden sarcasm.

Chelsea silently thanked him for it, and for changing the topic to one he wanted to discuss. The others went along with the aide, though Audrey looked disappointed.

Chelsea turned to Steve. "Sorry," she said quietly.

He smiled and patted her hand. His hand was large and perfectly sculpted. Chelsea smiled back at him, right up into his dark ember eyes.

And she knew, even before she snuck a peek, that his father was watching them. Once again there was that obvious look of approval.

The soup was cleared away and the crabs brought out. A heap of steamed ones, crusty with lip-buzzing Old Bay seasoning, were dumped at each end of the table. Mallets were handed around, and everyone started prying and banging. It was a relief to Chelsea to concentrate on pulling apart her crabs.

She noticed that Steve took his apart with great precision and piled the discarded parts quite neatly inside the apron of the shell. She started to straighten her own pile, and Judith laughed.

"That's why he put you next to me. Another garbage-pile girl. Ignore him," she said, flicking her head toward her brother. "I mean, I don't know why he doesn't just staple the claws on and stick them back in the ocean."

Chelsea laughed.

"He's too concerned with appearances," Judith said, "but you already know that."

Chelsea glanced up at Steve. She knew that the way he looked was important to him; there was a certain elegance about the way he dressed. But appearances were important to most people who were visual artists.

"You do know *that*?" Judith repeated uncertainly. She was looking at Steve now, and he returned her gaze, but Chelsea couldn't read the messages they were sending each other.

Chelsea shrugged. "So he's concerned with appearances."

Judith glanced at Chelsea once more, frowning a little. Then she turned back to Steve and shook her head at him. Steve remained silent. Reaching for another crab, he focused all his attention on it.

At the other end of the table, the talk was still business.

"We're going to be looking at the legislation on immigration this week," said Kenneth.

"Those laws need tightening," said Andy.

"Perhaps," said Hamilton.

"More like a thorough revision," said Susannah. "You don't have to live on the Mexican border to know that. Even Ocean City has pockets of illegals."

"Why is everyone so threatened by them?" Chelsea asked.

The question from her end of the table surprised everyone, including herself.

"Don't be naive," said Kenneth. "They're taking up jobs that belong to Americans."

"Usually the jobs are menial," Chelsea pointed out.

"We need every kind of job there is!" the aide insisted. "And they are costing us more than that. They are uninsured and they don't pay taxes. We pay for them and their needs."

"But if we made them legal," Chelsea replied, "they *would* pay taxes."

"Point!" said Hamilton.

Chelsea went on. "It just seems to me that all Americans came here that way, and—"

"I don't know how your ancestors came," Kenneth said sharply, "but mine were packed like animals and shipped."

Chelsea bit her lip. She hated getting into discussions like this. Usually she slunk away from controversy. But all she could think of was how Connor deserved an education, and a job, and a chance to use his gifts. Now she had done it, said something that was quite politically incorrect at a congressman's table.

Hamilton caught her eye and winked. "I know what you're thinking. Don't you decide to make this your last Sunday dinner here. The rest of us are used to Kenneth, and you'll grow used to him too."

Then Susannah stepped in to change the subject. Chelsea, wishing she could crawl under the growing pile of crab shells, sat quietly and ate.

At the end of the evening, as everyone was leaving, Hamilton told her twice that he hoped they would see her again.

When the door finally closed behind the Washingtonians, Chelsea let out a sigh of relief.

"My father liked you," Steve said.

Chelsea shook her head. "I think your father is simply a gentleman. Everything that came out of my mouth came out wrong."

He laughed. "Don't worry, I sound wrong to him all the time. And the fact is, he still liked you. You're a very attractive woman."

Chelsea tried to read Steve's dark eyes but couldn't.

"And what if he knew I was married? *You* know that, don't you?"

He smiled and put his arm loosely around her.

"Mmm-hmm. But being married doesn't make you any less attractive, any less sexy. Some—some guy will be lucky enough to finally win your heart, whether it's Connor or somebody else."

She looked up at him, this hunk, this sensitive artist that she had all to herself in an apartment by the sea. *My Condo Lover.* Every girl's dream. "You're gay, aren't you?"

"Yes. And I do apologize, Chelsea. I thought you knew before I asked you over. I didn't mean to lead you on."

"But you did mean to lead your father on."

He nodded.

"And you think you can continue to?"

"As long as he wants to be led, yes."

"Judith—"

"Has always known."

"Your mom?"

"She suspects. Maybe she knows. Chelsea"—his eyes had grown wary—"don't try to get me to come out to them. I can't do it yet. I just can't."

She sighed, then nodded. "I don't know whether to laugh or cry, or pound on you," she said.

"You've been lovely," he replied.

Then he drove her home. When they arrived, he hopped out of the car quickly to open her door for her.

"His light is on," he observed.

"How did you know which window was Connor's?"

"Tosh told me. You remember Tosh, the T.A. your brother ran away with."

Chelsea laughed.

"Shall I strut a bit and talk loudly until we see the curtains move? Then we can crowd into the shadows, and Connor won't be able to tell what's going on."

Chelsea smiled and reached up for Steve's face. She kissed him lightly on the cheek. "You don't need to put on any more shows tonight, and neither do I."

Then she hurried inside.

The living room was dark, with long rectangles of moonlight coming in from the deck windows. Chelsea was about to walk through to the deck. Then she heard the noises. The room was occupied. But the occupants were too busy to notice that she was there.

Smiling to herself, Chelsea tiptoed past them—Roan and Bo, making out on the couch.

SEVENTEEN

With great reluctance, Marta had let go of Dominic. She was in her chair again, earthbound, rolling along the boardwalk, wondering what she had done wrong.

Had she misread him? No. His kiss had been long and thirsty. But he had pulled away suddenly and had offered her no clue as to why. All she knew was that there was such an energy in her now, she was afraid it would work itself into a fury. She was afraid she'd lose her control and drag him kicking and screaming from that silent, dark world he kept retreating to.

She had to get rid of the energy.

"I have to race, Dominic."

"What?"

"I have to go fast. Fast!" She started wheeling north.

He stood flat-footed for a moment, then chased after her.

"Where are we going?"

"Other end of the boardwalk," she said, picking up speed. "Race you there!"

"It's another mile."

"Mile and a half!" she shouted over her shoulder.

Her arms worked, her lungs sucked down salty air, the wind pulled back her hair. She liked it, the hot and cold waves. She liked sweating, then shivering with the wind. She was moving fast, but she saved a little for the end. They'd fly the final quarter of a mile. She was sure she could beat him.

She did. She watched with some amusement as Dominic plodded the last twenty yards.

He sat down wearily on a bench next to her. "Is this what you always do when you're in your best clothes and have eaten a full-course dinner?" he asked.

Marta wiped the perspiration off her face, sat back, and smiled.

"This is what we do when you kiss me the way you kissed me, then pull away. Dominic, am I kidding myself? Didn't you want to kiss me?"

He looked at her and she knew that he did. And he still wanted to. What was it that haunted him so? Was he afraid of loving a girl with sticks for legs?

"Do you wish you hadn't fallen for me?"

Her question startled him. He dropped his head.

"That's it, isn't it? You have fallen for me, as I have for you. Only you hate yourself for it, for getting involved with—with a crip."

He closed his eyes. The pain was apparent in every muscle of his face. "I hate myself," he admitted.

"So," Marta said. "So." She swallowed hard. "That's how it is. I don't know why I'm so dense sometimes. I guess because I wanted so badly for it to be otherwise. But don't worry, Dominic, I won't make you any more miserable. We all have to decide what we can live with and what we can't."

He looked up at her, his eyes tunnels of night.

"I only wish *I* could hate you for how you feel," she said. "But I can't. I"—she laughed, choking back the tears—"I don't know where all the Salgado fury has gone to. No doubt it will come back to me. It can be quite useful, you know. In any case, I am sorry you fell in love and are so miserable for it. I hope you fall again for someone who's right for you."

Then she turned her wheelchair toward the ramp leading off the boardwalk.

"Marta. Marta!"

"What?" she said stiffly.

"You don't know why I hate myself."

She spun her chair around. "Let me guess.

Because I have a rag doll's legs and that sickens you? Or perhaps it's just that you can't help pitying people like me. Maybe it's because you owe somebody somewhere some debt and will be moving on—I like that excuse best. That's the one I've been holding on to. But really, it doesn't matter, because whatever the reason or excuse, I know you won't be staying around."

He walked over to her, and she forced herself to continue to face him, to keep her hands on the arms of her chair when all she wanted to do was wheel away from him.

He crouched down and took her hands in his. He kissed them gently, reverently.

"You're breaking my heart," she said.

He let go.

"Now you're breaking it again."

His face tightened, and she could barely stand to look at him. Then Dominic slipped off his tie and began to unbutton his shirt. Marta stared at his fingers, fascinated by them as they slowly undid each button.

Then he opened his shirt and she saw it, the snake of her most frightening dreams, the blue snake head with the grinning skull between its fangs.

She reached out and touched the tattoo, then pulled her hand away quickly. "One of them."

"One of them," said Dominic.

"You knew who I was all along."

"Yes," he said. His voice was low and strangled.

"And you were there that day?"

"Yes."

Tears ran down his face now. She was sorry for his pain. She was sorry, but she had to go on.

"And where were you standing?" she asked. "Help me picture it."

"I was standing across from the boy whose bullet struck and killed Christina."

"I see."

"My bullet struck you."

Marta didn't breathe, didn't move. The ocean itself stood still, or so it seemed. Then her mind arched with the blow as her body had seven years before. She felt the explosion in her, not once now, but over and over again, and she gritted her teeth, trying to keep herself upright in her chair.

"I am sorry." He breathed it as much as said it.

She couldn't see his face. She didn't want to see it. "You shattered my spine," she said. "Then my heart. Is there anything else you'd like from me?"

He didn't answer.

"Perhaps a dose of forgiveness?" she said bitterly.

"I would never expect you to forgive me," Dominic said.

Marta left him there. She wanted to shriek,

she wanted to cry hard, hard enough to bring the stars streaming down, and she would have wept for him as well as herself—except her heart, like her little-girl legs, recoiling from the blow, had gone suddenly numb.

EIGHTEEN

"I don't want to leave," Kate said with a sigh.

David's house was a snug little bungalow, an old shingled place whose shutters had weathered to a soft gray. Built long before anything stood north of Ocean City, it was still isolated, with state land on one side and the edge of the airfield on the other. David had added a deck that ran all the way around the house, and that was where Kate stood now, leaning against the railing, looking straight out toward the ocean. The moon cast a web of silver over the black water. It had been a perfect night. Tosh came up behind her and put his arms around her, loosely cradling her.

"I don't want to leave, Tosh."

"We don't have to," he said.

"Well, not till David gets home—"

"David's staying with Grace tonight," he told her.

"Is he?"

"That was part of our arrangement." Tosh rested the side of his face against Kate's. "We have all night to walk on the beach, to build a campfire, to dance under the stars—"

At that, they both laughed. Beneath a long note with instructions on everything from lighting the oven to jiggling the toilet handle, David had left them a stack of old LPs. They were collector's items, music he designated "croon and spoon tunes." He had also left them a dozen roses and myriad candles stuck in soda bottles. They had lit them all.

"If that doesn't sound exciting enough for you—" Tosh began.

"Yes?"

"We could play with Teddy."

"Forget it," Kate replied with a shudder.

The last line of David's note, "Teddy has been fed," had sent them on a hunt that ended at a terrarium next to David's bed, where Teddy the tarantula lived.

"You don't suppose he's smart enough to know how to get out, do you?" Kate asked now.

"My guess is he won't try anything until the deepest, darkest part of the night."

She squirmed at the thought, and Tosh tightened his arms around her. His body felt so good wrapped around hers.

"Mmm," she murmured.

"Mmm?" Tosh repeated. "You like the idea of meeting a hairy spider as big as your fist in the middle of the night, perhaps in your bed? I always knew you were a woman of exotic tastes."

She laughed. "I wasn't thinking about *Teddy*." In the middle of the night and perhaps in my bed, she added silently.

"Who were you thinking about?"

"Who?" she mocked.

"That's what I asked."

Kate leaned back against him. "You. You are such a good friend to me, Tosh. You listen so well. You're always there for me."

"And I always will be, Kate, there for you and no one else."

She turned to face Tosh. His eyes burned intensely blue. He touched her wrist, with just one finger, rubbing it ever so gently. "So, how is my Kate doing?"

"Fine," she said softly. "Never better, I think."

"You've had a rough time," he said.

"That time is past," she replied.

His fingers curled around one wrist, then the other. She could feel the heat in his hands, and she wanted to feel it all over.

She tilted her mouth up to him. He bent his head swiftly toward hers, but then, to her surprise, he laughed. He took Kate's right hand and wrapped it around his back. He brought the other hand up and began to dance with her, slow dancing, the old-fashioned way.

She longed to kiss him, but he continued to dance her around the deck, all the way around the outside of the house, his body sinuous against hers. He danced her into the living room and through the door to the bedroom.

Then he laid her gently across the bed. She pulled his head down toward her, longing for the touch of his lips against hers, but he kissed her hands instead. Then he kissed her knees, which were bare under her short skirt. She pulled his head up to her face again, opening her mouth, but he laughed and nuzzled her ear, then let his lips drifted down her neck till she thought she would scream with wanting him.

At last he gave her his mouth. He gave her long, deep kisses, each kiss making her ask for another.

Then she slid her hand beneath the waist of her skirt and found what she needed. It wouldn't have stayed taped much longer, she thought. How Justin would have laughed, to see where she kept a condom.

But Tosh wasn't laughing anymore. He was watching her and tracing her, trembling with the touch of her, as she undressed.

"Not far now," the old man said. "I could drive this road turned around backward with my eyes closed."

The young man smiled. So could he.

"I see this here bridge in my sleep," the truck driver continued as his eighteen-wheeler rumbled over it.

Me too, thought the passenger, though it's usually from underneath.

"Raleigh to Ocean City, Ocean City to Raleigh. Most of my life on this road. All the interesting things I ever thought, I thought on this road. Why, if they could hook my head into some kind of machine that would type out all my thoughts and dreams while driving this road, I'd be a famous author, like, you know, what's his name, his books got made into movies and all."

The passenger didn't reply right away. He was distracted by the town, the little houses, the dimly lit shops. "Faulkner?" he guessed. It was an author whose name he had filed away some time ago.

"That's it. Saw him on a talk show once, on my day off."

"I think Faulkner's dead," said the passenger.

"That Oprah, she gets all kinds."

The passenger smiled.

"And you know, you can never tell about people. You read the tabloids? You'd be surprised just how many people come back from the dead these days."

The young man turned to look at the driver. "I suppose it would seem that way."

"Any particular place you want to get dropped?"

"Actually, here's fine," said the passenger, picking up his knapsack from the floor of the cab. They were in the lower part of town; it would be a short walk back to the bay. "I'll leave the peanuts with you."

"Sure now? You know where to find a meal?" the driver asked. "Some pretty young woman expecting you?"

"Don't worry about me," he replied, climbing out of the cab. "I know my way around here."

Then Justin slammed the door, and the trucker roared off.

"But I'm not sure the pretty woman's expecting me."